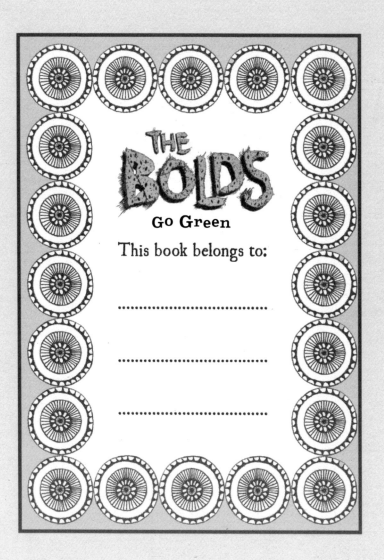

THE BOLDS

Go Green

This book belongs to:

....

....

....

Go Green

Look out for other books
in the series:

THE BOLDS

Go Green

By
Julian Clary

Illustrated by
David Roberts

Andersen Press
London

First published in 2021 by
Andersen Press Limited
20 Vauxhall Bridge Road London SW1V 2SA UK
Vijverlaan 48, 3062 HL, Rotterdam, Nederland
www.andersenpress.co.uk

2 4 6 8 10 9 7 5 3 1

British Library Cataloguing in Publication Data available.

ISBN 978 1 83913 051 9

Printed and bound in Great Britain by Clays Ltd, Elcograf S.p.A.

For
Charlie and Harriet

JC

For
Kirsten Grant

DR

Chapter

Would you believe me if I said I had never done anything **wrong**? It's true! I am as good as gold. (Unless we count that time I scratched 'JULIAN CLARY WOZ HERE!' on my school desk with a compass. But really, I was only stating a fact as I woz there. And as things have turned out and I am now a **famous** writer of children's books, that desk with my autograph on will be worth a LOT of money, I imagine. So there.)

But lately I've been wondering . . . is it possible to do something right, but still be wrong?

Suppose the person you were sitting next to at school was miserable because their hamster had died and you told them their hamster had gone to Heaven or you offered to buy them a new one. Then the teacher told you off because you were talking in class and gave you a detention. Were you doing something right or wrong? It isn't always an easy question to answer, is it?

I was once in Regent's Park's formal flower garden, admiring the red-hot pokers (or *kniphofia*, if you're posh) and a woman sitting on a bench was distraught because the silk scarf, which her daughter had given her for Christmas, had blown away and landed in the middle of a rosebed. I retrieved it for her, even though it meant walking on the grass and ignoring the Do Not Walk on the Grass sign.

The woman was very grateful and thanked me with tears in her eyes. I felt sure I had done the right thing. But the park-keeper saw me on the grass and was quite angry about it. Veins standing out on his forehead and all that sort of thing.

'That sign is there for a reason, young man!' he shouted. (I *was* young at the time, before you say anything.)

So, tell me, what should I have done? Tell the woman she couldn't have her scarf back? Or break the park rules and reunite her with her precious top-of-the-range neckwear?

I don't know the answer. But it may be that this conflict between right and wrong is what this book will be about. (I don't know yet as I've only just started writing it. More news on this as I get it.) Let's talk about the Bolds.

At Number 41 Fairfield Road, the twins, Bobby and Betty Bold, had just got home from school with their best friend Minnie.

'How was the last day of term?' asked Mrs Bold – they were now on their Easter break.

'Well, we've got some important news,' said Betty. 'Bobby and I are going to be Green Monitors for the whole school next term!'

'Gosh, that's wonderful,' said Mrs Bold, a little surprised. Her children, delightful as they were, didn't often get chosen for positions of responsibility. They were, as she well knew, a little inclined to silliness and easily distracted.

'We have to go on patrol!' Bobby informed her. 'We check that no one has thrown rubbish on the floor, or left taps dripping, or lights on when they leave a room.'

'And if we find anyone doing anything wrong, or not green in any way, we will be forced to arrest them!' said Betty, her eyes glinting in anticipation.

'Really?' exclaimed Mrs Bold. 'And do you know how to arrest someone?'

'Of course!' said Bobby. 'We restrain the culprit, subdue them if necessary and march them to the headteacher's office quick sharp.'

Mrs Bold looked a little worried about this, but as it wasn't going to happen till next term, she decided to think about it another time.

'How was the *rest* of your last day?' she asked.

'It was great!' said Bobby. 'We didn't do proper lessons. No maths, or anything awful like that.'

'Oh, that's good,' said his mother. 'What did you do instead?'

'We watched a film about Planet Earth!' said Betty.

'That sounds interesting. What did you learn?' asked Mrs Bold, pouring sparkling lemonade into three tumblers.

'Well,' began Minnie, 'first we learned that there are millions of planets in the universe – but Planet Earth is special.'

'Because we live here?' asked Mrs Bold.

'Er, yes. But we can only live here because Earth has just the right combination of water, atmosphere and climate,' explained Minnie seriously.

'And jokes!' said Mr Bold, who'd just arrived home from his shift at the Christmas cracker factory where he worked. 'Which reminds me ...'

Betty giggled at her father's joke but then her face became quite serious. 'But now the planet is suffering,' she informed her parents. 'Global warming. Climate change. Pollution. Rising sea levels.'

'And all because of humans,' said Bobby, looking accusingly at Minnie.

'Sorry,' she said. 'But I, for one, am very keen that we make things better while we still can.'

'Well, what's to be *done*?' asked Mrs Bold, slicing up a delicious home-made chocolate cake.

'That's why Green Monitors are so important,' said Bobby proudly. 'We're here to help and remind you.'

'We must turn off electrical devices when they're not needed and reduce our carbon footprint,' said Betty.

8

'Don't waste water!' said Bobby.

'Reuse and recycle!' chipped in Minnie. 'And grow more plants to eat.'

'And enjoy nature,' said Betty.

'This all sounds much like the way we hyenas live already,' pondered Mr Bold.

'Hmmm,' said Mrs Bold. 'Yes, it does sound a lot like the hyena way of life. But we do eat rather a lot of meat.'

'What's wrong with that?' asked her husband.

'Well, it's not like we hunt and catch our own meat these days, dear. We buy most of it from the supermarket and I read somewhere that the meat industry is the worst cause of climate change in the world.'

'Really? How?' asked Mr Bold.

'Well, it's all the **burps** and ʃarts the cows do,' said Mrs Bold. 'They release lots of methane gas into the atmosphere and that's what's heating up the planet and melting the polar ice caps.'

Mr Bold rolled on his back, laughing. 'Cow burps! Cow farts?' he said.

But Mrs Bold looked at him crossly. 'Do get up, dear. We have a gueʃt.'

'Is that really true, Mum?' asked Betty. 'Cow burps are causing climate change?'

'Yes, it is,' said her mother.

(She's right. If you don't believe her or me, look it up. Cow burps are a major factor in climate change.)

'So I've been thinking,' continued Mrs Bold. 'From now on we shall go veggie twice a week.'

'Go veggie?' asked Mr Bold. 'What does that mean? No chops?'

'Precisely. And tonight we'll have a cheese and vegetable pasta bake,' his wife informed him. 'It will be delicious.'

'I hope so,' said Mr Bold, looking doubtful.

'I hope so too,' said Mrs Bold. 'Because *you're* doing the cooking.'

'Oh,' said Mr Bold.

Just then the door opened and in wandered Uncle Tony with Mr McNumpty, their next-door neighbour, back from a walk in Bushy Park.

'Afternoon, everyone,' said Mr McNumpty. 'School finished now for the holidays, has it?'

'Yes,' confirmed the children.

'And the twins have just

been telling us they've been made Green Monitors,' said their mother proudly.

'Green Monitors, eh!' said Uncle Tony, not really sure what a Green Monitor was.

'How about you, Nigel?' Mr Bold asked Mr McNumpty. 'Do you fancy going green?'

'But I've just bought myself a new blue coat. It would clash horribly . . . you know what they say: blue and green should never be seen.'

'No, silly. Go green, as in save the planet!' cried Bobby.

'Oh, I see. All right then. I'm all for saving the planet. Will it take long? Only I want to go to the library and it closes at five.'

'Well, according to the children we all have to do our bit. Er, grow vegetables, mind our footprints and stop emitting gas.'

13

Mr McNumpty patted his tummy thoughtfully. 'Ahem. No more sprouts for me then.'

'At school we now have a green area,' Betty informed the adults. 'Some of it's a wild meadow and some of it is for growing vegetables. And there's a beehive, a worm hotel and an ant farm.'

'Beehive!' said Mr McNumpty.

'Yes, bees are easy to keep and do lots of good for the environment,' said Betty.

'You could have one in your garden, Mr McNumpty,' suggested Bobby.

'I could indeed, old chap. And then I could help myself to some honey every now and then. Excellent idea! Bears, as you know, are quite partial to honey,' said Mr McNumpty, licking his lips.

'There, now I've turned green. What fun!'

'What can *I* do?' asked Uncle Tony.

'Well, we're all going to be doing our bit in this house by eating less meat,' Mrs Bold informed him.

'Oh,' he said sadly. 'But I love meat.'

'And we must never drop litter and always clear up our streets,' said Bobby. 'In fact we did some of that on our way home from school, didn't we, Sis?'

There was something in the tone of Bobby's voice that worried Mrs Bold.

'And what did you do exactly, Bobby?' she asked with a growing sense of foreboding.

The twins looked at each other and giggled. Minnie nudged them. 'I told you not to!'

'We noticed that the front garden at Number 10 needed some attention, that's all,' said Betty innocently.

'Number 10? That's the Binghams' house. They're so easily upset,' exclaimed Mrs Bold.

'And?' asked Mr Bold.

'And so we gave it some,' said Bobby. 'That's all.'

'Some attention?' frowned his mother.

'Some liquid fertiliser . . .' said Bobby. The words hung in the air.

Mrs Bold rubbed her forehead. 'Oh no. You'd better give me more details, please.'

'Well, we were walking along Fairfield Road, picking up bits of litter. In the front garden of Number 10 we spotted a sweet wrapper,' explained Betty. 'It seemed a shame to leave it there, polluting our lovely street.'

'Quite right!' said Mr Bold.

'So we jumped over the wall to get it,' continued Bobby.

'I didn't. I knew it would lead to trouble,' said Minnie.

'I picked up the sweet wrapper and then I noticed the marigolds in the flowerbed were wilting,' said Bobby.

'It *is* quite a hot day out there,' mused Uncle Tony.

'And as it happened I needed a wee.' Bobby's voice became strangely quiet. Minnie shook her head.

'So . . .'

'You *didn't*, Bobby!' cried Mrs Bold.

'Yes. I did.'

'Good for the marigolds and good for the planet,' said Betty helpfully. 'Much better than using the loo and flushing it away.'

'Think of the gallons of water you've saved!' said Mr Bold, patting his son on the back affectionately. 'Well done, my son!'

Mr McNumpty helped himself to a French fancy. 'Oh well, as long as Mr and Mrs Bingham didn't see you, I guess there's no harm done.'

'Er, they *might* have seen me,' said Bobby.

'Oh dear. "Might have"?' asked Mrs Bold.

'The net curtains twitched,' recalled Minnie. 'And there was a high-pitched scream.'

'Maybe they were watching something scary on television?' said Mr Bold reasonably. 'They are quite a nervous couple.'

'Then the window opened and Mr Bingham shook his fist and shouted something.'

'What did he shout?'

'We couldn't hear because we ran away,' said Betty.

'The correct response to being shouted at,' said Mr Bold approvingly.

Mrs Bold put her head in her hands.

Just then, Uncle Tony changed the subject by producing a postcard. 'Oh,' he said. 'I nearly forgot. This was on the doormat.'

'How exciting,' said Mrs Bold, taking it and reading it quickly.

'Who's it from?' asked the twins.

'See if you can guess,' said Mrs Bold, holding up the card with an excited glint in her eyes. 'I'll give you a clue. What's this?'

The twins and Minnie leaned over to look at the photo on the card.

'Triangles!' said Bobby.

'No, dear,' said Mrs Bold. 'Think wonders of the world.'

'The Pyramids!' cried Minnie.

'Correct! Well done, Minnie. And where are the Pyramids?'

'Egypt,' said Betty confidently.

'Not necessarily,' warned Minnie. 'We shouldn't forget the Great Pyramid of Cholula in Mexico.'

Bobby rolled his eyes. Sometimes Minnie was too clever for her own good these days.

Then Minnie peered closely at the postcard. 'No. Betty is right. These are Egyptian! The Giza Pyramid Complex, which includes the Great Sphinx.'

'Thank you,' said Betty.

'Well done, Sis,' said Bobby, nudging her so her slice of cake slid across her face. Betty's extra-long tongue wiped it clean in a second.

'And who might be writing to us Bolds from Egypt?' asked Mrs Bold with a knowing look.

Can you guess? Well, let's read on and find out.

Chapter

At this point I'd better interrupt to explain something. You know the Bolds aren't people, right? They are hyenas from Africa, living disguised as humans in a very pleasant house in Teddington. Everyone knows that by now, surely? This is the sixth book about them, after all.

But you never know. The thing about books is we have no idea where they will end up. I write them and shops sell them or people buy them online. They get read. But then what? They sit on bookshelves or get lent to friends. Or maybe they live in libraries and go to various different homes, back and forth. Books, it seems to me, can have adventures just like people. You might leave this book on the bus, for example. Someone might pick it up and take it home with them. Then what? Maybe they take it on holiday and leave it behind. On the beach, maybe. The book might be swept away when the tide comes in, float out to sea and get washed up on a desert island. On that island lives a lonely castaway who hasn't had the pleasure of reading a decent book for years and years. He or she dries the book out and reads it with much excitement. But if it happened to be this book, and they hadn't read any of the others in the series, they wouldn't know, would they, about the Bolds' unusual origins. You see what I mean? As the author I have a responsibility to cover every eventuality. I can't assume that my reader knows all about the Bolds. That bit about Betty's long tongue licking up the cake, for example, would be most confusing if you didn't know she was a hyena. In fact I should probably have mentioned it earlier but I didn't get round to it. Soz.

So, to be clear (in case this is being read by someone on a desert island), Fred and Amelia Bold are wild, laughing hyenas who left the Serengeti Plain to start a new life in Teddington. They learned to talk like humans, wear clothes, and walk on their hind legs. Mr Bold now has a job writing the jokes that go in Christmas crackers, and Mrs Bold makes very unusual hats out of discarded rubbish,

like old flowerpots
or birds' nests,
which she sells
at her stall
in Teddington
market. Mr and

Mrs Bold have twins called Betty and Bobby
who go to school. There they met Minnie,
who is one of the only people who knows their
hyena secret. Minnie has promised never to
tell. The Bold family live at 41 Fairfield Road,
Teddington. Also resident is an elderly hyena
called Uncle Tony, who they rescued in an
earlier book from a nearby safari park, along

with his companion,
Miranda, who is a cute
little marmoset monkey.
Tony takes Miranda
out and about in her
doll's pram for a walk
most days.

Tony is very friendly with the neighbour at Number 39, Mr Nigel McNumpty (who happens to be a grizzly bear – hence his interest in honey). They often go for ice cream  together and enjoy a nice game of dominoes afterwards.

The Bolds are a happy family, who laugh almost all the time – because they are hyenas. They also rub their bottoms on gateposts and enjoy scavenging in the local bins, but I won't dwell on that here. More importantly they like to help other animals to live as humans too. They have been very successful at this, as you'll know if you've read the previous books. (If you haven't, and you're a castaway in the middle of an ocean somewhere, I hope you get rescued soon, so you can have a haircut and eat sweets and read all the other Bolds books.) There are too many animal 'students' helped by the Bolds to list here, but just take it from me. Crocodiles, racehorses, a poodle, an otter, a sheep and many, many others, have all been successfully tutored in humans' funny ways at Number 41 Fairfield Road and then sent off to live new, exciting lives disguised as humans.

Which brings us neatly back to the story in hand. The postcard featuring the Pyramids of Giza: it had come from someone the Bolds know and love . . . someone out in the world, living their dream thanks to the Bolds.

Let's get on, for goodness' sake! There's nothing worse than trying to read a nice story and the author keeps droning on and on about some old nonsense.

'Who do you think sent us the postcard then?' repeated Mrs Bold, still holding it up. 'Who do we know, who now lives in Egypt?'

'Sheila the crocodile!' said Bobby.

'No, not Sheila. Sheila lives wild, swimming up and down the Nile,' his mother reminded him. 'She could hardly climb out the river and go to a newsagent's to buy a postcard and a stamp, then borrow a pen from somewhere and pop it in the post, could she?'

'Stupid!' said Betty.

'Stupid, yourself!' said Bobby crossly. 'Who is it from then, if you're so clever?'

There was a pensive silence.

'Can we have a clue, please?' asked Minnie.

'OK,' said Mrs Bold. She held out her arms like she was onstage, picked up a mini Swiss roll and held it to her mouth as if it were a microphone and wailed: '*Je ne regrette rien!*'

Bobby and Betty both gave a rather hyena-ish whoop of excitement while Minnie clapped her hands with delight.

'Fifi!' they all cried together.

'Fifi the French poodle!' exclaimed Betty.

'The very same,' said her mother.

'How is she?' asked Bobby.

'What does she say?' enquired Minnie.

Fifi, you may or may not know, came to stay with the Bolds a while back. With their help – not to mention her own natural talent – she made the change from howling hound to international singing sensation. She was now living the dream, singing songs in the cabaret lounge onboard a luxury cruise ship in Egypt.

'Well, children,' laughed Mrs Bold. 'Fifi's postcard is

very exciting and rather mysterious at the same time. I'll read it to you, shall I?'

'Yes, please!'

Mrs Bold cleared her throat.

Bonjour ma famille!

C'est moi, Fifi Lampadaire, writing to you from my cruise ship. We have docked here for a day so the tourists can visit the Giza Pyramids. I have so much news. I am singing as wonderfully as ever and receiving beaucoup d'attention from everyone, in particular the adorable Samir . . . he is très romantique! I will tell you all about him when I see you. Yes, I am coming home to visit you all! A star returns to her humble roots!

'Fifi is coming back!' cried Betty and all three children began to jump up and down with excitement.

'Hurrah!' said Bobby. 'Can't wait to see her.'

'She has a boyfriend too! When does she get here?' asked Minnie.

'Well, let me finish reading and you'll see,' said Mrs Bold reasonably. She continued:

You are not to worry, but . . . I have un petit problème . . . I will be with you next Saturday. I will need a quiet bedroom and LOTS of your delicious home cooking.

Au revoir, mes chéries,
Fifi xxx

'Wow,' said Betty.

'I wonder what her little problem is?' contemplated Minnie.

'Just a furball, I expect,' said Bobby.

'Egyptian fleas?' wondered Betty. 'We'd better get some flea powder.'

'Er, we have some already,' said Mrs Bold, looking very slightly embarrassed. 'Those of us with fur need the occasional treatment. Saves scratching in public.'

'I can't imagine a great star like Fifi having fleas,' pondered Minnie. 'I mean, Shirley Bassey doesn't have nits, does she?'

'Not as far as we know, dear,' agreed Mrs Bold. 'Although she has worked with the Pet Shop Boys.'

'We'd better get the spare room ready,' said Betty. 'I think it will be quiet enough for her.'

'Oh Lord,' gulped Mrs Bold. 'Quiet, yes – but clean enough? I don't think so! It's filthy in there. And full of junk.'

She was right: the Bolds' spare bedroom had been host to all manner of animals recently: foxes, otters, a goose – and was decidedly whiffy as a consequence.

'We're on holiday now,' said Betty. 'We can all help get it ready for Fifi!'

'And remember what we've been learning at school,' added Minnie excitedly.

The twins looked up and said together:

'Reduce, reuse, recycle!'

'Well done,' said Minnie primly.

'Yes,' said Bobby. 'We don't just CHUCK stuff out. We find a new home for it.'

Mrs Bold thought about the piles of clothes, shoes, saucepans, bits of wood and half-chewed hosepipes and goodness knows what else that was in the spare room.

'This will be a challenge,' she said. 'But I'm sure my Green Monitors will be up to it. We'll start tomorrow, shall we? Perhaps I can make some new hats out of some of it?'

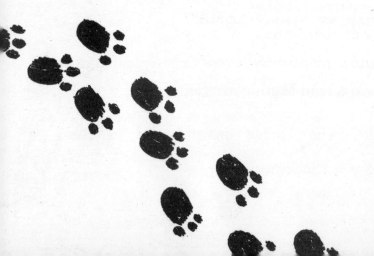

Chapter

The next day the clean-up of the spare bedroom began in earnest. Of course, Minnie came round to help. Mrs Bold was busy making several new hats – Easter was coming up and she was feeling very creative. Easter was always a busy time at her market stall and she was determined to have plenty of amazing, unusual bonnets for her customers.

'You three go upstairs and get started,' said Mrs Bold, handing them some bin liners, a dustpan and brush, a bucket of warm, soapy water and some squirty cleaning stuff.

'We haven't had a guest in there since Jeffrey the ape man and I'm afraid it has become rather a dumping ground for all sorts of bits and pieces.' She looked a little worried.

'But I'm sure you'll sort it out. I'm just downstairs if you need me. I had a look in there this morning and you're going to be quite busy. Several of our students left their calling cards behind – much like *you* did, Bobby, in the Binghams' front garden.'

Bobby giggled.

'And the smell of fox is quite delicious. But unfortunately Fifi won't like it, so you'll have to scrub the floor and probably the walls to get rid of it.'

'We'll open the windows too,' said Minnie, wrinkling her nose.

'Call me when you need a drink or a snack.'

Bobby, Betty and Minnie went upstairs and opened the door to the spare room. Except it wouldn't open very far – there were so many things in there. Eventually the three friends managed to squeeze in.

'Oh dear!' said Minnie.

'Wow!' said Bobby.

'Oops!' said Betty.

The Bolds, as you know, are always taking in other animals and either giving them shelter or, more usually, teaching them how to live disguised as humans. They have to learn how to walk and talk like humans, wear clothes – and most importantly, to use the toilet. This can be quite difficult, as the sights and smells in the spare room showed. But apart from *that* mess, there were piles of dirty clothes, chewed-up bits of wood, and old bones and toys strewn everywhere. A mound of shredded books, broken walking sticks, cardboard boxes, old shoes, broken hangers, hosepipes, saucepans, an old bicycle and who knows what else, reached almost to the ceiling. What was left of the curtains was torn and hanging in shreds – almost as if some creature or other had been swinging around from them. Worse still, a pair of foxes had lived in that room for several months and built an earth den there. Although the earth had been used later to make mud bonnets for Mrs Bold's hats, quite a lot of it had been left behind. The windows were so dirty you could hardly see through them. Several flies buzzed around the rubbish, clearly cross at being disturbed.

'Right then,' said Minnie, rolling up her sleeves. 'Let's get started. We need to sort things into various piles,' she added decisively. 'Reuse, recycle and, er . . .'

'Restore?' offered Bobby.

'Something like that. And we'll need another pile for charity shop stuff. That's four piles. I'll pick things out, pass them to you, Betty, and Bobby will put them in the right pile. Here goes.'

And so the clean-up began. It was tough, dirty work and everything had to be looked at and – in the twins' case – sniffed and nibbled. It was difficult to know where to begin, so Minnie started with the mound in front of her. A black handle was sticking out of a pile of clothes, so she tugged at it until it came free.

'A frying pan!' said Minnie, handing it to Betty. 'That should clean up with a bit of scrubbing. Reuse, I think!'

Betty took the pan and sniffed it. 'Hmmm. Bacon and eggs. Yes, reuse pile, please, Bobs.' She passed the pan to her brother.

Bobby sniffed it too, then couldn't help but lick it. 'Smoky bacon,' he concluded. 'Free-range eggs. Scrambled!' He had another slurp then placed the frying pan down on the small area of floor that was still available.

'Next – an old newspaper. Rather soiled,' said Minnie, quickly passing it to Betty. 'Recycle.'

'Ugh!' said Betty, tossing it up in the air for Bobby to catch. Bobby caught it and sniffed the air.

'Craig the wild boar,' announced Bobby. 'He never *did* get the hang of loo paper.' He shook his head and placed the newspaper in a new pile next to the frying pan.

Meanwhile Minnie tugged at a green trouser leg until eventually an old pair of tracksuit bottoms emerged.

'Charity shop?' she wondered.

'Ah!' said Betty. 'I remember when Uncle Tony wore these. Bless!' She handed them to Bobby. 'I wonder if he'd like them back?'

'I don't think he'd get into them any more,' said Bobby, tugging at the elastic waistband. 'He's put on a few pounds. All that ice cream in the park with Mr McNumpty!'

'Charity shop pile then,' decided Betty.

'Righto!' said Bobby. Now there was no

space anywhere to start a charity shop pile so Bobby decided it was best to throw the tracksuit bottoms over his shoulder and hope for the best.

Had they had time to glance out of the window they might have seen there was quite a lot of activity going on next door at Number 39 as well. Mr McNumpty and Uncle Tony were in the garden there, dressed from head to toe in protective clothing, setting up a brand-new beehive. They'd only just released the queen bee and her drones into their new home, but already Mr McNumpty was looking forward to some reward.

'Do you think there will be any honey to eat by this evening?'

'Er, no, Nigel,' said Uncle Tony. 'First the queen needs to lay lots of eggs, which then hatch into worker bees who will go and collect the pollen. Takes all summer, you know, before you get any honey.'

'Oh well,' said Mr McNumpty. 'I'll be patient then. Nice to know I'm doing my bit for the planet.'

Back at Number 41 the big clean-up of the spare room continued. Every item was perused by the twins and Minnie, and its new destiny decided upon. It was filthy, tiring work, but the three friends didn't mind: they were together, having fun, and helping the environment along the way. After an hour and a half they had made quite a dent in the huge mountain. Minnie wiped her forehead with the back of her hand.

'Shall we have a break? I think a drink and a biscuit is called for.'

'Yes!' agreed the twins. It was only now that Minnie and Betty turned round, expecting to see four neat piles. Instead, Bobby was knee-deep in all the things they had just sorted through, all in as much of a muddle as before.

'What . . . on . . . earth?' said Minnie.

'What have you done with all the stuff, Bobby?' asked Betty.

'Where are the different piles?' said Minnie.

Bobby looked around him. 'Er, well, I think I got a bit confused.'

'There's still as much mess – it's just in a different place!' cried Minnie crossly.

'Now we can hardly get out of the room!' said Betty.

Bobby scratched his head. 'I'm sorry,' he said. 'I didn't realise. I was having fun.'

Betty smiled at her brother. 'To be fair, so was I.'

'But now we've got to start all over again!' said a bewildered Minnie.

'So? That just means we can have even *more* fun!' reasoned Bobby.

'What a WASTE of time!' said Minnie, shaking her head. But she couldn't help but smile.

Bobby wondered what was best to do. Then he realised he should do what his dad did in situations like this. Tell a joke!

I used to work in a recycling centre, crushing cans.

Did you really?

Yes. But I had to give it up. It was soda pressing. Ha ha!

By now all three of them were laughing so much, the time they had wasted didn't seem to matter and they decided to go down to the kitchen for a drink of something fizzy and a chocolate biscuit.

'How's it going?' asked Mrs Bold when she saw them.

But the children were laughing too much to reply.

Chapter

When Mrs Bold was told about the funny business in the bedroom she thought it best to give some more detailed instructions to avoid more time-wasting.

'It's a lovely day, so why not bring everything from the spare room down to the garden, then we can sort it out properly?'

So that is what happened. Mr Bold waited in the garden (Mrs Bold was halfway through her Easter hat collection) as Bobby, Betty and Minnie delivered the contents of the spare room, armful by armful. Then they picked through each item and decided its fate. Next, Miranda the marmoset monkey placed it in the appropriate pile. This time the piles were in separate areas, well away from each other, so there would be no more mix-ups. This took the whole afternoon.

'Well done, children!' said Mrs Bold. 'Now before we start the next stage of the proceedings – taking stuff to the recycling centre or the charity shop – I want to have a look through to see if there is anything that might be useful for my hats.'

First she found a chewed plastic penguin. 'This is nice,' she declared. 'I'm sure I can repair it!'

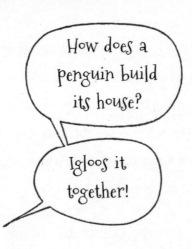

How does a penguin build its house?

Igloos it together!

'And plastic flowers! Always useful,' continued Mrs Bold, tugging at some stalks.

What kind of flowers grow on your face?

Tu-lips!

Some bright yellow plastic plates in the reuse pile caught Mrs Bold's eye. 'Hmmm . . . very cheerful. I'll take these too.'

Knock, knock.'

Who's there?

Dishes.

Dishes who?

Dishes a nice place you've got here!

Mrs Bold chose a few more **random** items, and then the twins and Minnie helped Mr Bold load up the little blue Honda with things for the recycling centre.

'Now all these clothes,' said Mrs Bold to the children, 'can go to the charity shop around the corner. Fold them up neatly and let's put them in the wheelbarrow and take them there.' There were quite a lot of clothes and the wheelbarrow was piled high, but they just about all fitted.

'We'd better be careful,' said Minnie. 'I'll lead the way and Bobby and Betty can take one handle each.'

As Mrs Bold was busy finishing off her hats and Mr Bold was at the recycling centre, Minnie and the twins asked if they could go on their own. The charity shop wasn't far and there were no roads to cross.

Mrs Bold wondered if this was a good idea. 'You will go straight there and straight back?' she asked.

'Of course, Mum!' said Betty.

'Promise!' said Bobby.

'And you'll stick together?'

'Absolutely!'

'And not talk to strangers?'

'It's fine, Mum, we know all about stranger danger. We are nearly ten, after all!'

'I'll make sure they don't get up to any

mischief, Mrs Bold,' said Minnie in her most sensible voice.

'Oh, OK then,' said Mrs Bold. 'I suppose it will be all right for you to go without me . . .' And she gave the three friends permission to go to the charity shop.

What is your opinion about this expedition? Do you think the twins and Minnie should be allowed to go out unsupervised? It's a tricky one, isn't it? Knowing the twins and Minnie as I do, I wouldn't call them untrustworthy. Prone to unusual happenings, or magnets for fun and the occasional spot of bother, perhaps, but not untrustworthy, never! I'd trust them with my wallet, although they might eat it. But however we look at it, it is unlikely that this trip to the charity shop will pass without incident. Two young hyena pups and a wheelbarrow full of second-hand clothes out unaccompanied on the wild streets of Teddington sounds like a recipe for disaster to me . . . But there comes a time for every parent when they have to test the water and let their little ones out of their sight, so that was what Mrs Bold did that afternoon. I suppose the best course of action is just to get on and tell you what happened. The truth is it is something you'd never guess anyway. It is my prediction, therefore, that this *whole* paragraph of speculation and rumination will be edited out by someone from my publishers wearing a severe haircut and novelty earrings that look like throat lozenges. A red line will be put through it, I dare say, and the word 'padding' scribbled in the margin. (Words like 'rumination' are usually considered unsuitable for children. I don't know why. It's been one of my favourite words since I was about nine. We'll see, won't we? Sigh.) Onwards!

'What could possibly go wrong?' Mrs Bold

asked herself as she watched the young trio trundle the heavily laden wheelbarrow through the side gate and onto a sunny Fairfield Road.

'Turn left!' called Minnie when they reached the pavement.

'I can't see a thing!' said Bobby, playing for time as he reminded himself which was his left and which was his right. (The fur on his left paw had a brown smudge on it, so he had a surreptitious look.) Working together Bobby and Betty managed the left turn and the trio began making steady, if wobbly, progress along the pavement in the direction of the high street, when suddenly Minnie – walking a few metres ahead – called out: 'Warning! Pothole danger imminent!'

But it was too late. The front wheel of the barrow fell into the crack between the paving stones, causing the whole thing to stop

suddenly and crash to one side. The precarious pile of assorted clothes teetered then fell silently to the ground.

'Nooo!' cried Minnie.

'It's not *our* fault,' said Betty. 'You didn't give us enough warning.'

'Sorry. I didn't notice it in time,' said Minnie.

'Come on, let's just get it all back on,' said Bobby.

'I don't think there's time to fold it again, do you?' said Betty. 'The charity shop closes soon. If we get there too late we'll have to wheel everything back home to Number 41 again, and I don't fancy that.'

'OK,' said Minnie. 'Let's pile it back on, then we can fold it when we get there.' All three of them scooped up armfuls of garments and piled them onto the wheelbarrow, which now looked like a colourful pile of rags.

'Ready?' asked Minnie, resuming her position as head of the expedition. 'Let's move steadily forward.' Minnie was rather enjoying being in charge. She felt quite important and imagined she was a policewoman escorting a wide load down a busy motorway. 'Steady as she goes!' she called.

Unfortunately, at this stage, the twins had started to get a bit bored. It was tiring work and they couldn't see a thing, their paws were sore and their minds had begun to wander, understandably. Bobby sighed.

'How much further, Sis?' he asked despondently.

'Dunno, Bruv.'

'It's all right for Minnie, waving people

out of the way and giving orders, but we're doing all the hard work.'

'I've had enough.'

'Me too!'

'Let's liven things up, shall we?'

'Yes!' said Bobby, a glint in his eye. 'Let's try hopping on one leg for a bit!' Betty thought this was a marvellous idea and on the count of three both pups began to hop – slowly at first, then faster and faster and even faster.

Minnie glanced behind her and saw the precious cargo had started pulsating and bouncing.

'Whoa there!' she said. 'What's going on, you two?'

'This is much more fun!' giggled Bobby.

'It is too,' agreed Betty. 'But we haven't got much time, remember. Do you think we should speed up?'

'Running hops? Oh yes, let's!' agreed Bobby.

Suddenly the juddering wheelbarrow was speeding towards Minnie and she had no option but to jump out of the way, over a low brick wall, landing with a crash in the carefully manicured marigold bed of Number 10. The Binghams'. As she got to her feet and brushed the dirt and garish orange petals from her dress, the wheelbarrow sped past her like a runaway train.

'STOP! STOP!' she cried, but the twins were having too much fun to hear and on they went.

Minnie was just getting to her feet when Mr Bingham flew out of his front door in his dressing gown (he liked to have a nice bath in

65

the afternoon before watching *Tipping Point*) and grabbed Minnie by the arm.

'You hooligan!' he shrieked. 'Look what you've done to my flowerbed!'

'So sorry,' said Minnie. 'I'll explain later, but I can't stop now. I'm in charge of that wheelbarrow, you see.'

'What wheelbarrow?' asked Mr Bingham suspiciously, tightening his grip. 'I want your name and address, young lady. I've a good mind to call the police.'

An alarmed Mrs Bingham now appeared by her husband's side, holding a neatly folded fluffy white towel and some bath salts. 'Careful, Richard,' she said, her voice trembling. 'She's probably part of a gang. We're caught up in a turf war. I've read about this sort of thing in the paper. Oh, look at my marigolds!'

'It was an accident. I'm really sorry. I had to jump out of the way. The wheelbarrow—'

'She's crazy!' cried Mrs Bingham. 'Lock her in the shed while I call 999!'

Minnie decided the only thing to do was run for it. 'Sorry!' She shrugged at the Binghams and ran to catch up with Bobby and Betty.

The twins, meanwhile, unaware that Minnie was no longer there to guide them along Fairfield Road, assumed that their way ahead was clear and safe and so their hopping just got faster and faster and, it has to be said, more and more fun. As they flew down the road, the pile of charity shop clothes hopped too and one by one items flew up in the air and landed, scattered across the pavement, gutter, gates, gardens and trees of Fairfield Road, until the whole street looked as if a jumble sale had somehow exploded.

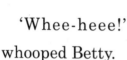

'Whee-heee!'
whooped Betty.

'This is more fun than fun!' cackled Bobby.

But as they built up
speed, hopping on one
leg soon became impossible and before
they knew it the twins were running, then
sprinting, as fast as they could. That part
of Fairfield Road sloped downwards and the
twins began to lose control.

'Oh-er!' said Betty as she lost her
grip on the wheelbarrow handle. The
contraption veered suddenly towards
the road and Bobby let go too.

'Oops!' he gasped. Bobby and Betty clasped
each other as they helplessly watched the
wheelbarrow crash into a lamp post and
somersault into the air, landing with a

crunch on top of a shiny silver Range Rover. The last few items of clothing formed a kind of multi-coloured fabric Catherine wheel in the sky – a pair of Mr Bold's old long johns waved to them from on top of the lamp post and

Mrs Bold's sports bra was last seen wrapped around the head of a passing motorcyclist.

The twins stood, panting on the pavement, covering their mouths with SHOCK. It took a few moments for them to realise there was only one thing for it: to laugh. And so they did. And, as is the way with hyenas, the laughter reached a cackling crescendo, the effort of which caused the twins to keel over. By the time Minnie had escaped from the Binghams' clutches they were both on their backs, arms and legs waving helplessly in the air.

'Bobby! Betty!' panted Minnie. 'Pull yourselves together – look at the clothes everywhere! We need to get them all back before we get into more trouble.'

Just then a puzzled Mr McNumpty and Uncle Tony appeared, on their way home from their trip to the library. Uncle Tony, as usual, was pushing Miranda, the tiny marmoset monkey, in her doll's pram.

'Well, well, what's going on here then, eh?' asked Uncle Tony.

'Found a new way to dry your washing?' chuckled Mr McNumpty. 'By throwing it up in the air all down the street?'

'We're supposed to be taking these clothes to the charity shop,' explained Betty, getting to her feet.

'But it all went a bit wrong,' added Bobby.

'So I see,' said Uncle Tony.

'Wheelybarrow on top of car-car!' observed Miranda.

'Yikes,' said Minnie. 'Let's get it off before the owner notices.'

Mr McNumpty, being tall and strong, lifted it off with one hand. Fortunately there was a roof rack on top of the Range Rover that had prevented any damage. He placed the wheelbarrow back on the pavement and everyone went about gathering the escaped clothes. Helpfully, Miranda climbed nimbly up the lamp post to retrieve the long johns.

'All done!' said Minnie at last.

'We'll be off home then,' concluded Mr McNumpty. 'Glad to have been of assistance.'

'Would you mind not mentioning this to Mum, please?' asked Betty.

'She wasn't sure if we could be trusted out on our own,' added Bobby.

Mr McNumpty tapped the side of his nose. 'Mum's the word, eh?' he winked.

'Thank you!' said the twins.

'Now let's try again,' said Minnie. 'Sensibly, this time.'

Mr McNumpty checked his watch. 'Chop, chop,' he said. 'Charity shop closes soon, you know.'

'Right. We're off!' said Bobby, waving goodbye.

You'd think that would be enough nonsense for one day, wouldn't you? But you'd be wrong. These are the Bolds we're dealing with here, remember. Nonsense is their middle name.

Chapter 5

So here is what happened next. Our intrepid trio made it safely to the corner of the high street, miraculously keeping the wheelbarrow upright and all the clothes where they should be. In fact, they were only a hundred metres from their destination when fate stepped in. Sitting huddled on the pavement outside the greengrocer's was an elderly figure, wrapped from head to toe in rags. As the twins and Minnie passed, she held out a gloved hand, palm upwards.

'Please help me,' she said in a whisper.

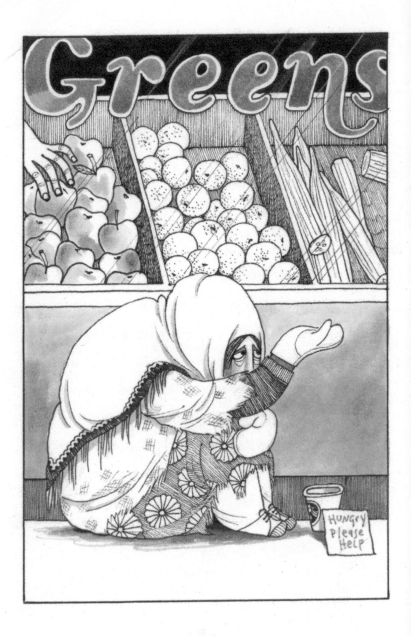

'Stop!' ordered Minnie and the three youngsters approached her.

'Could you spare a few pence?' she asked. Minnie peered at the face shrouded in its hood. Her skin looked dirty and grey.

'Oh, you poor thing!' she said. 'But I'm afraid we don't have any money.'

The old lady stared at them with kind, watery eyes.

'Ah, you are children. I didn't realise. Please don't worry then. A man gave me five pence a couple of hours ago. So nice of him. People are very kind in Teddington.'

'Five pence? Is that all you have?' asked Bobby.

'Well, yes, so far,' the old lady said.

'We don't have any money. But would you

like some clothes?' asked Betty, gesturing towards the wheelbarrow. 'Bound to be something here that fits you.'

'Oh.' The old lady peered at the mound of clothes. 'Thank you. It does get rather chilly at night on the streets.'

'Is that where you sleep? On the streets?' asked Minnie.

'Yes, dear,' said the woman. 'I do.' She shivered slightly.

'That's awful,' said Bobby.

'It's not so bad if I've had something to eat,' replied the woman.

'Well, our mum and dad will help you, I'm sure,' said Betty.

'Deffo!' said Bobby emphatically. 'We're the Bolds. We love helping people.'

The old lady's eyes widened slightly. 'The Bolds, you say? Well, if you're sure?'

'Absolutely. We'll take you to ours for something to eat. What would you like?'

'I only eat two things. Ants or cucumbers.'

The twins looked at each other, then at Minnie, their eyebrows raised in surprise.

'Really?!' exclaimed Minnie. 'That's an unusual diet . . .'

The old lady shrugged.

'Well, we don't live far away. Come back with us now. I expect there is a cucumber in the fridge,' offered Betty. 'And you can choose some clothes too.'

'We were on our way to the charity shop with these, but *you* can have them instead,' said Bobby.

The old lady got slowly to her feet. 'Looks very comfy,' she said, eyeing the mound of clothes. 'I'll rest myself on these, if you don't mind?' And she shuffled towards the wheelbarrow and lowered herself on top. 'Ready when you are!' she said. 'My name is Annika, by the way.'

'Right then, Annika. Let's turn around,' said Minnie, more than a little nonplussed.

And so it was that the twins and Minnie's expedition to the charity shop ended twenty minutes later with their return to 41 Fairfield Road, still with all the clothes and the added addition of an old lady called Annika, who only ate cucumbers and ants, riding on top of the wheelbarrow.

Chapter 6

Mrs Bold heard the children returning through the side gate and put down the hat she was making (a bonnet festooned with giant butterflies made from the soles of old shoes, brightly painted and sprinkled with glitter – a special commission for the Teddington Pride parade, happening later that summer) and went to meet them. Her heart melted at the sight of poor Annika and she helped the old lady out of the wheelbarrow and into the kitchen.

'Make yourself at home, my dear,' she said, putting the kettle on.

'We met her on the high street,' said Betty.

'She is very hungry and has nowhere to live!' explained Bobby. 'So we brought her here.'

'You did the right thing,' said Mrs Bold, proud of her caring, compassionate children. 'Everyone is welcome at the Bolds' house. For as long as they need to be here.'

'We were just about to deliver the clothes to the charity shop. But Annika could have some of them, couldn't she?' added Minnie. 'So we brought them all back again.'

'Yes, Minnie dear. Go direct to the needy. Cut out the middle man, as it were. Although she might not want *all* of them. Now, Annika, would you like a nice cup of tea?'

'You're very kind, all of you. Just a glass of water if it isn't too much trouble,' Annika said, and then pushed her hood off and gave

her head a shake. She had a long, blunt nose,
a very wrinkled forehead and big, round eyes.
But almost as big as her head were her long,
pinkish ears, which stood rather high on
her head.

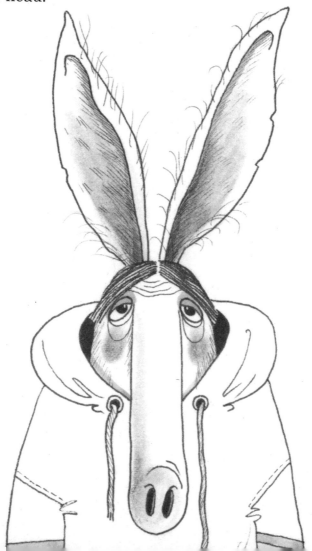

The twins and Minnie couldn't help but stare, until Mrs Bold frowned meaningfully at them.

'You three go and sort through the clothes and see what might be suitable for Annika. I'll get her something to eat. Would you like a sandwich, dear, or something more substantial? You look as if you haven't eaten properly for days!'

Annika smiled weakly and peered at Mrs Bold.

'Your delightful daughter mentioned that there might be a cucumber in your fridge?'

'A cucumber?' repeated Mrs Bold, opening the

fridge. 'Er, I expect we have such a thing. Is that what you fancy? On a slice of granary bread?'

'No, thank you. Just as it comes. And ants. I eat ants.'

Mrs Bold didn't flinch, but began slicing on a chopping board. She studied Annika as she did so and nodded to herself.

'Have you come far, Annika?'

'It's a long story. I'll explain later,' said the visitor, her nose twitching at the sight and smell of the freshly cut gourd.

'Of course,' said Mrs Bold knowingly. 'You tuck into this and I'll send the children to gather some ants for you. Bobby? Betty? Get some ants, please!'

'Thank you, Mrs Bold.'

'Ah,' said Mrs Bold, nodding. 'You know

my name. You have heard about us Bolds, I suspect. Is that why you came to Teddington? To find us?'

Annika was enjoying the delicious fresh cucumber, and wiped a drop of juice from her chin. She only nodded as her mouth was full.

The Bolds, as you know, have helped lots of animals over the years. Their door is always open to waifs and strays and word of their kindness has spread far and wide across the animal kingdom. Try saying 'The Bolds!' to your pet cat, dog or guinea pig and I guarantee their pupils will dilate and a look of respect will cross their faces. In fact I once visited the zoo in Beijing in China and I asked a giant panda if she had heard of the Bolds. She barked excitedly and then did a triple back somersault, which the keeper said he'd never witnessed before, ever!

Mrs Bold sat down next to her visitor and said: 'Well, I am glad you found us, Annika, and I want you to know you are very welcome here. We've never had an aardvark come to visit before. You're quite a rarity!'

Yes, that's right: Annika wasn't an old lady at all, but an aardvark! Do you know what an aardvark looks like? We can pause for a moment while you google it if you like . . . Curious looking, aren't they? All big ears and long snout. A bit like the Prince of Wales but without the cufflinks. They live in burrows and eat only two things: ants and cucumbers. (The Prince of Wales would have cucumber sandwiches but probably isn't keen on ants. I can't say for sure, as posh people eat some strange things, like caviar and oysters.)

Aardvarks have been sadly absent from children's storybooks as far as I can discover and it is high time this was rectified.

'Yes, Mrs Bold, I am indeed an aardvark,' agreed Annika. 'Well spotted!'

'Please, call me Amelia,' said Mrs Bold. 'So would you like to tell me your story? And how can we Bolds help you?'

Annika finished the last of her cucumber with a satisfied slurp. Then she took a deep breath and began to speak.

'I'm a gentle aardvark – most of us are. But I'm very shy, Amelia; I like a quiet life. Sleeping is important to me. A few hours a night, snuffling about for ants, a quiet meander in the moonlight, and I'm quite happy. But that wasn't what was expected of me. Born in captivity, I found myself at a place called Shorthop Zoo. Someone there came up with the bright idea of "The VIP Aarvark Experience", if you please.' Annika gave a little shudder.

'What did that entail?' asked Mrs Bold.

'Oh, it was frightful. People. Groups of ten or so brought into my pen every fifteen minutes. All day every day. They'd paid quite a lot and they wanted their money's worth. I was stroked and prodded, squealed at and photographed. Some aardvarks might like that sort of thing, but I didn't. It was torture. I just wanted to be left alone. But the worst of it was each visitor was allowed to feed me a handful of termites. If I didn't play along I'd get nothing to eat!'

'Oh, you poor thing!' exclaimed Mrs Bold.

'I'm so glad you understand. I don't think
the zookeepers did. I'm sure they are animal
lovers and wouldn't deliberately do anything
to upset me, but I wasn't suited to the work,
you see? I'm not a performer by nature. I had
to sit up and beg, lick my food from these
stupid sticks they'd wave in front of me. They'd
pat my back and sometimes scratch me. I'm
not being unkind, but humans aren't always
the gentlest or, if I may say, the cleanest of
creatures. And it was relentless. One
group out, the next
group in.'

Mrs Bold shook her head. 'Awful for you.'

'Intolerable!' agreed Annika.

'Did you have other aardvarks with you to keep you company?'

'I did not. A while back I was presented with a "mate" called Adrian, but we didn't get on. He had, er, amorous intentions, but he had bad breath and his eyes were too close together.' Annika grimaced at the memory. 'As if I'd couple up with just any old aardvark! We weren't compatible and that was that. He was sent to Chester Zoo after a few months and good luck to him.'

'Just as well,' nodded Mrs Bold, and Annika took another deep breath.

'I am very grateful to you for listening, Amelia. I feel better sharing all this with someone who understands. Thank you.'

'The trouble with humans is they don't stop to think what an animal might need to be happy. They can be a little thoughtless sometimes.'

'You're telling me! And so my life, such as it was, continued. Day after endless day. I was unhappy and it was torture. Groups of excited humans treating me as if I were some sort of toy for their amusement. And I was so tired – we are nocturnal animals – I just wanted to sleep all day but that was not possible. They wanted me awake and on show.'

'It's a wonder you didn't get ill.'

'I did, Amelia. I did. My mental well-being was seriously affected. I just curled up in a ball one day and refused to carry on.'

'Good for you!'

'The VIP visitors were most upset and

demanded their money back. The keepers were rather cross because they were losing all that business, but I wouldn't budge. I just couldn't.'

'You were on strike!'

'Yes! The vet was sent for and I was given a thorough examination. Nothing physically wrong with me, of course. But I was given a vitamin injection to buck me up.'

'Ouch!'

'Ouch indeed. Most unpleasant. Aardvarks are very thick-skinned and she had to use a very big needle.'

'Then what?'

'Well, this is where my story gets happier, I'm pleased to say. I was sent to the sick bay. Under observation.'

'At least you could get some rest!'

'Yes. Peace and quiet at last. In the next pen to me was another poorly fellow called Charlie. A skunk.'

'Don't they smell terrible?'

'Only when they're threatened or distressed.'

'What was he in the hospital for?'

'Well, that's the thing. He didn't like being leered at by the general public any more than I did. But he had a way to make his feelings known.'

'Spraying!'

'Yes. Correct. If he didn't

like the look of a human being who came to look at him he simply turned around and sprayed his pungent scent all over them!'

'Ugh!'

Annika paused for a chuckle and of course Mrs Bold joined in.

'Awful of me but I'd love to have seen that!'

'The best one was a lady in a real fox fur coat. Covered her from head to toe, apparently!'

'Serves her right!' said Mrs Bold, punching the air with her paw. 'Well done, Charlie! Bullseye!'

'So Charlie and I became firm friends, united by our mutual dislike of being objects of amusement for the paying public. We whispered long into the night about our desire to escape from Shorthop. We thought no one could hear us, but we were wrong!'

'Who was listening?'

'There was a fruit bat with a damaged wing in the sick bay too. She heard everything.'

'Bats do have exceptionally good hearing,' observed Mrs Bold.

'Quite. Big ginger thing, like a flying fox. Fergie, she was called. We thought she was hanging upside down asleep, but she was eavesdropping.'

'No!'

'Yes, but fortunately she wanted to help and together the three of us hatched a plan. But we had to act fast. Fergie's wing was almost better and she would soon be transferred back to the bat enclosure.'

'What was the plan?'

'It was genius. Fergie had been born in the

Kakadu National Park in Australia. Eventually she'd flown to Cairns and taken up residence in a church tower with several other fruit bats. It was there that she'd met a nun called Sister Paulina.'

'Not Miss Paulina, our former student? The otter with a religious vocation?'

'Yes, the very same. She was doing missionary work there.'

'What a small world!'

'Sister Paulina told Fergie about you Bolds and all you had done for her.'

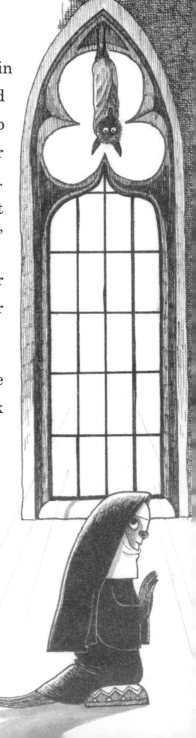

'Ah, that's nice of her. She was an exceptional student. I'm glad she is doing so well.'

'She prays for you every day.'

Mrs Bold felt tears brimming in her eyes.

'But how did Fergie end up at Shorthop?'

'Captured for some international fruit bat breeding programme,' explained Annika.

Mrs Bold shook her head.

'She was placed in Taronga Zoo in Sydney originally, then swapped for a couple of barn owls, apparently.'

Mrs Bold bristled. 'So sad!'

'Indeed. Fergie was quite put out. But back to her clever plan. Charlie and I had no idea how to escape from Shorthop or where we would go if we did. But Fergie suggested that

if we pooled our resources – flying, digging and, er, ʃprayiɳ smelly scent – we could get out of that place, surely. Then, once free, we'd make our way to you Bolds and freedom!'

'So how did you manage it? And where are Charlie and Fergie now?'

'I'll explain everything,' said Annika. 'I don't suppose you have another cucumber handy?'

Mrs Bold shook her head. 'I'm afraid not. But let me look in the cupboard. I think there is something similar.' She opened the larder and reached to the back to retrieve a glass jar. 'Yes! Just as I thought! Pickled ɡɦerkiɳs. Any good to you?'

'All part of the cucumber family, I suppose,' said Annika doubtfully. 'I'll try one.'

Mrs Bold unscrewed the jar, fished out a gherkin with a fork and passed it to Annika.

The aardvark sniffed it suspiciously then popped it sideways into her mouth and crunched it.

'Quite zingy!' she said, blinking with surprise. 'But lovely nevertheless.'

'Here, help yourself,' said Mrs Bold, tipping all the gherkins onto a plate for the visitor.

After three or four more gherkins, followed by a discreet burp, Annika resumed her tale. And what a remarkable tale it was.

Chapter

7

'We activated our plan two nights later,' continued Annika. 'There was only one member of staff on duty in the sick bay between the hours of eleven p.m. and eight a.m.: a rather grumpy veterinary nurse called Simon. I don't think he was very happy in his work. He never spoke to us kindly and he spent most of his time reading magazines or picking his nose. He was supposed to check on all the patients every hour but he rarely bothered. Just shouted "Shurrup!" if anyone made a noise.'

'He doesn't sound like a very nice or professional person!'

'No. He wasn't. There was an armadillo in with tummy trouble and he used to enjoy poking her with a pencil to make her roll up into a ball for his amusement.'

'Cruel!'

'Most unusual for a veterinary nurse. Most of them are animal lovers, kind and caring. But not this Simon.'

'He should be sacked!'

'That's what we thought. And that made it easier for us to carry out our plan. Just after two in the morning, as arranged by us, Charlie started coughing and wheezing and making as much noise as he could. Simon told him to "Shurrup!" and "Stop that racket!" several times but Charlie just turned up the volume.

'Eventually, Simon realised he had to actually do some nursing for a change, so he came and peered through the bars of the cage. "Darn thing. Not dying on me, are you?" he asked crossly. At this point Charlie went silent and lay on his side, eyes glazed, as if he were seriously ill. Simon then became worried – if an animal died on his watch he'd have some explaining to do. He got the keys out of his pocket, then put on some latex gloves. He opened the door and lifted the limp, lifeless skunk out of his cage and placed him on the examination table.

'"How do you check the pulse on a skunk, for goodness' sake?" he mumbled, scratching his head. And then, quick as a flash, Charlie came to life, jumped up on all fours, turned and sprayed Simon full in the face from his scent glands.'

'Another bullseye!' said Mrs Bold, clapping her paws together with delight.

'Yes!' agreed Annika. 'Simon reeled back, choking and covering his eyes. I must say the smell was very strong! Simon couldn't see a thing, and was writhing on the floor. Then, without hesitation, Charlie jumped off the table, grabbed the keys and opened my cage and then Fergie's.'

'Then what?'

'Well. The main exit to the sick bay could only be opened with a security code, which we didn't have, but the door to the exercise yard wasn't locked – we knew this. Simon was supposed to lock it but he never did because he was too lazy. So into the yard we went.'

'Did you climb over the fence?'

'Impossible. It was completely covered with wire mesh to keep the bats and other flying animals in. So I had to dig our way out.' She held up her powerful front paws. 'With these!'

'Very impressive,' said Mrs Bold admiringly.

'Thank you. Aardvarks are built for digging through termite hills. Plus we live in burrows, so it's second nature to us. I managed to dig a channel wide enough for me, Charlie and Fergie to squeeze through fairly quickly. Just before the alarm bells went off . . .'

'No!' cried Mrs Bold. 'Simon had recovered?'

'It seems so,' said Annika through gritted teeth. 'But we were through and into the zoo grounds.'

'Bravo!'

'We ran and hid as quickly as we could. Shorthop is over nine thousand acres big, so we knew that if luck was on our side we'd be able to lie low somewhere.'

'Could you dig your way out of the zoo grounds too?'

'No way. It's all properly fortified. They have lions and all sorts there. No, digging wasn't going to work. Meanwhile there were sirens and alarms, and security guards rushing about carrying stun guns. We were hiding out at the back of the reptile house, hidden by some shrubbery but Land Rovers with searchlights were being used and we didn't stand a chance.'

'Awful!' said Mrs Bold, biting her claws with worry. 'So what happened?'

'We tried to stay calm and stick to our plan.'

'Which was?'

'Fergie. Her damaged wing was mended. She would pick us up and fly us over the wall!'

'Ah! I'd almost forgotten Fergie is a fruit bat!'

'But she couldn't carry us both at the same time. She'd never be able to take off. Charlie insisted I be first. We said a hurried "Goodbye and good luck! See you on the other side!" and waited for the searchlight to clear, then we took our chance. Fergie grasped me by the

ears and began to flap. I'm no lightweight and I was worried I'd be too heavy for her. But with a lot of flapping, and with me running as fast as I could on the ground, we eventually took off. It wasn't easy gaining enough height. We had to circle round a couple of times. I could hear poor Fergie puffing and panting but finally we cleared the wall with centimetres to spare, the bright beam of the searchlight hard on our heels. Then we landed with a crunch in some woods. We'd made it.'

'Free at last!' said Mrs Bold, giving Annika a hug.

'Freedom is the most wonderful feeling. Like nothing else!'

'I know, dear,' said Mrs Bold nodding sagely. 'It is the most important thing in the world for every living thing. But I want to know: did Fergie go straight back to get Charlie?'

Annika stood up and shuffled to the window where she stood gazing out in silence for a few moments.

'She did,' she said quietly. 'But that's the last time I saw her. She never came back. I don't know what happened to her or Charlie.'

Chapter

The thoughtful silence between aardvark and hyena was interrupted by the return of Bobby, Betty and Minnie. They were all streaked with mud from head to toe.

'Sorry we were so long,' said Betty cheerfully.

'Catching ants is great fun!' contributed Bobby.

'The hosepipe was involved,' added Minnie with a grin.

'Really, dear?' said Mrs Bold, casting her eye over the three sets of muddy footprints on her kitchen floor.

'Did you get me some ants?' asked Annika hopefully.

'Yes!' said Minnie proudly, holding out a jam jar. 'Six!'

'Six?' repeated Annika, sounding a little forlorn.

'Did you want more then?' questioned Bobby.

'Well, the thing is – and I don't want to sound greedy – do you know how many ants a day the average aardvark eats?'

'Er, is it more than six?' said Betty.

'Yes. Fifty thousand!' announced Annika. Everyone looked stunned. 'They're only small!'

'I suppose that's true,' said Minnie. 'Hardly bigger than crumbs.'

'And I'm quite a big girl,' nodded Annika.

'Where can we get that many ants from?' pondered Bobby.

'I know!' shouted Betty. 'Bobby and Minnie, come with me!'

Her brother and friend did as they were told and followed Betty outside.

'What are we going to carry fifty thousand ants in?' wondered Betty.

'The wheelbarrow?' suggested Bobby.

'No, they'll crawl out, silly.'

Minnie looked around the garden. 'Dustbin!' she cried.

'That'll do it,' said Betty. 'We'll have to empty it first, though.'

After some discussion it was agreed that,

as it was an emergency, it would be OK to tip the rubbish over the fence into Mr McNumpty's garden.

'It will only be there for a little while. He probably won't even notice,' reasoned Betty.

'He'll quite understand once we explain, I'm sure,' said Bobby, emptying the full bin of rubbish over the dividing fence and giving it a shake.

'But where are we going to get the fifty thousand ants from?' asked Minnie, not unreasonably.

'School,' said Betty. 'The new ant farm, remember? I don't know how many are there, but there's a lot.'

'Are we going to have to count them all?' asked Bobby, looking worried. 'Only I'm not very good at counting over a hundred and it will take ages.'

'We'll just have to make an intelligent guess,' said Betty. 'Come on, let's go.'

The three ant hunters set out for school, carrying the large (now empty) bin between them. Minnie worried that they really shouldn't be going on the expedition alone, but Bobby pointed out they'd already been allowed to go to the charity shop that day without adult supervision.

115

'And look what happened then,' muttered Minnie.

When they got to the school the gates were locked for the holidays, but Bobby and Betty didn't see this as a problem.

'Come round the side,' said Bobby. 'There's a hole in the fence where we can slip through. I've used it before when I'm late for school and want to sneak in without being seen.'

Minnie was beginning to lose her nerve. 'We're going to get into trouble,' she said. 'This is burglary!'

'Oh, Minnie!' said Betty, stamping her foot. 'Don't be such a WUSS!'

'But it is!' insisted Minnie. 'We might get expelled!'

'Only if we get caught,' said Bobby. He

looked around to make sure no one was in earshot. 'Betty and I are hyenas, remember. We are clever and we are fast. We have excellent hearing and sense of smell. We can hide and pounce and scavenge and we always get what we want. And what we want is to feed a poor, starving aardvark. This is all perfectly reasonable in my opinion.'

'Er, OK then,' said Minnie, unconvinced. 'But I'm not a hyena, more's the pity. I might be more trouble than I'm worth. Why don't I wait here and keep lookout? If I think anyone is coming I'll whistle. Like this . . .' and she let out a tuneful whistle.

'Wowsers!' said Betty admiringly.

'Whistling is one of the few things hyenas can't do,' said Bobby. 'Here's the gap in the fence.' He peered about, then threw the bin over into the school grounds.

'I'll pretend I'm tying my shoelaces,' said Minnie, as the twins slipped through the gap.

Bobby and Betty looked around them. The empty school building was quiet and dark.

'Come on, Sis,' said Bobby in a whisper. 'The ant farm is round the back by the vegetable garden. Follow me.'

Why did the ant smell?

Because he didn't wear deodorANT!

Betty thought again as they crept across the playground.

What do you call an ant who skips school?

A truANT!

'Ha ha ha!' guffawed Bobby. 'Got any more?'

'Don't think so,' said Betty.

'I have,' said Bobby.

Where do ants go on holiday?

FrANTS!

What do you call the tallest ant in the world?

A giANT!

The twins were enjoying a good laugh, but Betty pulled herself together first.

'We'd better concentrate,' she said seriously. 'We can do some more ant jokes later.'

'Righto,' agreed Bobby.

The twins were at the door of a small shed, which housed both the ant and worm farms. 'It's in here!' Bobby declared excitedly.

Now, in case you don't know, the proper name for an ant farm is a formicarium, designed for the study of ant colonies. Those who study ants are called **myrmecologists**. These are long, complicated words which normally I wouldn't bother with as some people find them tedious. But just sometimes it's nice to know something that no one else knows. Ask a grown-up if they know the proper name for an ant farm and I guarantee they won't. But let's get back to the twins.

The shed door opened with a creak and they slipped inside with the empty dustbin. The shed was quiet and dark with a musty, earthy smell.

'We should have brought a torch with us,' said Betty.

'Shall I turn the light on?' asked Bobby. 'There's a switch here.'

'We hyenas can see in the dark, Bruv. Give it a minute and our eyes will adjust.'

To pass the time they told some more jokes.

How did Noah see in the dark?

He used floodlights!

Why were the middle ages called the dark ages?

Because there were too many knights!

Soon the darkness lifted and the twins could see the farms: the worm farm was a tall, square green plastic arrangement and not very interesting to look at. Betty sniffed.

'This one has worms in it. Shall we eat some?'

'We'd better not. We might get carried away,' replied Bobby sensibly.

'Wow, look at all these ants, though!'

The ant farm was two large sheets of see-through plastic with wavy trails and chambers going from top to bottom, a man-made copy of what goes on in an ant hill. Thousands of ants could be seen moving busily around, clambering over each other. There were nests and eggs and an awful lot of ant activity going on in all areas.

'But how are we going to get the ants out of

the farm and into the bin, so we can take them home for Annika?' wondered Betty. 'We can't pick fifty thousand up one by one.'

'I once left a half-sucked boiled sweet on the windowsill. When I went back for it half an hour later it was covered in ants,' said Bobby.

'Ugh!' said Betty. 'I hope you threw it away?'

'Er, no,' said Bobby. 'It was a lemon sherbet. My favourite.'

'So you ate it, ants and all?' laughed Betty, wrinkling her nose at the thought.

'Yup . . . ants taste a bit nutty.'

'I've got a toffee in my pocket!' remembered Betty. 'If I give it a bit of a chew and put it in the bin, maybe the ants will all come to investigate?'

'Great plan!' said Bobby.

It was a bit of a challenge for Betty to chew the delicious toffee and not swallow it afterwards, but she managed to resist. She popped it, glistening, in the bottom of the empty bin. She then placed the bin next to the ant farm, and Bobby opened the little door. The ants stopped what they were doing, waved their antennae around as if sniffing the air, then began, one by one, to march purposefully in the direction of the tasty toffee.

'It's working,' declared Betty.

'Look at them go!' said Bobby.

Soon the ants' silent march became an ant charge. Out of the farm they came, hundreds at a time, like a thick trail of pulsating molasses. The first ants to reach the toffee leaped on it with glee, covering it in no time. But they were soon jumped on by their comrades. The spot where the toffee was grew and grew as more

and more ants reached their destination. The twins looked on, amazed as the mass of ants swelled to the size of a tennis ball. Seconds later it was as big as a watermelon and still growing.

'The whole bin is going to be full of ants in a minute!' said Bobby, giving his sister a congratulatory slap on the back.

'We've done an excellent job of finding Annika's dinner. Mum will be pleased with us,' smiled Betty. The twins beamed at each other.

But the siblings' joy was rudely interrupted by a shrill whistle.

'Shhhh!' said Betty. 'Listen . . .' The whistle came again, sounding more urgent than before.

'That's Minnie's warning,' whispered Bobby. 'Someone must be coming!'

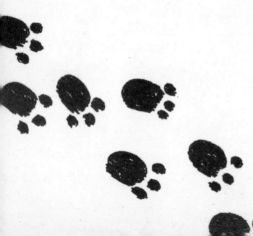

Chapter

'Quick. Close the ant-farm door and put the lid on the bin,' Betty whispered urgently. 'We've got to get out of here!'

'Sorry, ants. No toffee for you lot,' Bobby explained to the remaining ants, as he blocked their progress to the sticky treat in the bin.

Minnie was now whistling more or less constantly.

'Hurry!' said Betty, as she opened the shed door very slightly and peered out. 'Coast is clear!'

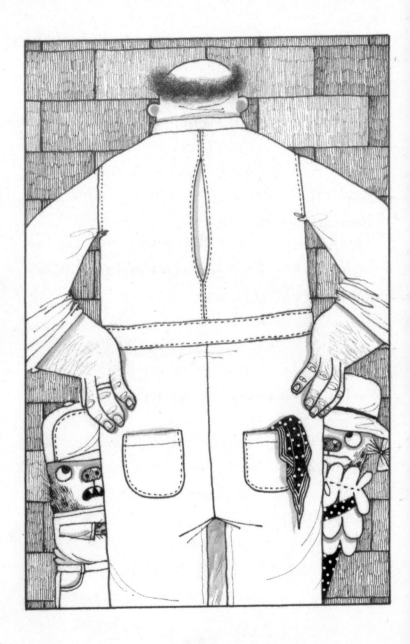

The two hyena pups slipped back into the playground. Carrying the bin between them, they made their way swiftly around the school building towards the gap in the fence.

'Hold it right there, you two!' boomed a loud, cross voice, and a large, rotund shadow loomed over the twins.

'Bobby and Betty Bold, I do believe . . . What exactly do you think you are up to?' asked Mr Herbert, the school caretaker. He was a big man and known as a 'no nonsense' character.

The twins froze. 'Ah, er, hello, Mr Herbert,' stammered Betty.

'We're not "up to" anything, honest!' said Bobby, playing for time while he tried to think of a believable excuse.

'Yes, you are,' stated Mr Herbert. 'Trouble follows you two around like a bad smell. You're

131

on school grounds in the school holidays when you've no business here. Carrying a dustbin, no less. What's in it, eh?'

'Nothing!' cried Betty.

'We always carry a bin around with us,' said Bobby desperately. 'Just in case.'

'In case of what, might I ask?' demanded the caretaker.

'In case we need to put some litter in it,' improvised Betty.

'Rubbish!' barked Mr Herbert.

'Exactly!' answered Bobby, rather pleased with himself. 'We're very green, you see. We're Green Monitors for next term and we are, er, getting some practice in. We pick up rubbish wherever we see it, don't we, Betty?'

'Oh yes,' nodded Betty. 'All day long.'

'Doing our bit for the community, you see.'

'No need to thank us – we do it because we care,' concluded Betty, attempting a saintly expression, which didn't come naturally.

'Good day to you,' added Bobby. 'We'll be off now.' The twins picked up the bin and hurried away from the caretaker.

'Not so fast!' said Mr Herbert, running after them and grabbing them each by the scruff of the neck. 'You haven't explained what you're doing on school property. This is a serious matter and I'm going to have to write a report and give it to the headteacher.'

'Er,' said Betty.

'Um . . .' said Bobby.

'You Bold twins are in big, big trouble!' said Mr Herbert, tightening his grip. 'You're coming with me.'

Just then he was interrupted by a familiar cackling laugh. Everyone turned to see Mr Bold bounding towards them.

'Dad!' cried the twins, giggling with relief.

'Mr Bold,' said Mr Herbert angrily. 'Can you please explain why—'

> Why is a school like an old bus?

> Because it's full of nuts and has a crank up front!

'Stop telling stupid jokes, Mr Bold!' demanded Mr Herbert, getting red in the face.

'Knock, knock!' continued Fred Bold.

'MR BOLD! BE QUIET!' boomed the caretaker, actually jumping up and down with frustration and anger.

Mr Bold did as requested, straightened his face and his hat and offered an innocent, questioning face. 'How can I help you, Mr Herbert?'

'I want an explanation, Mr Bold, and I want it NOW! WHY were your children found on school grounds carrying a large dustbin? Eh?'

'Yes, right,' smiled Mr Bold. 'An explanation, no problem . . .' He looked at Bobby and Betty, then at the bin, then back to Mr Herbert. 'Yes. Er. Yes. Hmmmm.' Mr Bold gazed at the sky, then at the trees swaying in the breeze, thinking hard.

'I'm waiting,' said Mr Herbert, tapping his foot impatiently.

'Got it!' said Mr Bold at last. 'It's the wind, you see,' he began. The twins looked at their father, confused.

'The wind?' repeated Mr Herbert, leaning forward and frowning.

'Yes, the wind. Awfully blowy today, isn't it?'

'What has the weather got to do with anything?'

'Well, we'd been to the recycling centre, you see, to empty the bin, which was full of rubbish. We Bolds are very green, you know.'

'Yes, I've heard,' said Mr Herbert flatly.

'We were on our way home, and the bin was on the roof of the car.'

'On the roof?' Mr Herbert asked suspiciously.

'Wouldn't fit inside. My little blue Honda is rather compact, don't you know. Anyway, we were driving past the school when there was a sudden gust of wind. The bin blew off, flew up in the air, over the school fence and landed here. Bobby and Betty – always such helpful children – offered to retrieve it while I parked the car. That's it. Perfectly innocent.'

Mr Herbert scratched his head. 'Er, I don't know about this,' he said. 'Sounds suspicious to me.'

'Nonsense!' cried Mr Bold. 'I can quite understand you jumping to the wrong conclusion. Spotting two youngsters in your school during the holidays, carrying a bin. Who wouldn't? A timely reminder to us all what an excellent school caretaker you are! As I was saying to Mrs Dobson, the headteacher, only the other week. Best in the business, you are, Mr Herbert.'

'Oh, am I? Thank you very much, Mr Bold. Very kind, I'm sure.' The caretaker was suddenly beaming with pride.

'Don't mention it. All sorted now. We'd better be off. Come on, kids!' said Mr Bold brightly. 'I'll help you with that naughty dustbin.'

And with a cheery wave, Mr Bold, Bobby and Betty swiftly left the school and went in search of Minnie. Once they were all safely in the car, Mr Bold told the twins they shouldn't have been breaking in to school.

'But we needed the ants for Annika!' said Betty.

'What else could we do?' asked Bobby.

'Annika?'

'An elderly, homeless lady we met on the high street,' explained Bobby. 'Only she's not an old lady really, she's an aardvark and a very hungry one.'

'I see. But you went out the house without

telling anyone. Your mother was worried sick when I got home from work.'

'Sorry, Dad,' apologised Betty.

'We didn't think,' said Bobby.

'And while we're at it, Mr McNumpty is most upset about the rubbish you tipped over his fence.'

'It was only for a little while. We'll clear it up when we get back. Promise.'

'Yes, you will. And maybe tidy up his garden too, to say sorry.'

It was unusual for Mr Bold to be cross with his children, and the journey back to Fairfield Road proceeded in silence.

'Dad?' asked Bobby eventually.

'Yes, son?' replied Mr Bold.

140

'How did you know where we were? Only, if you hadn't arrived when you did, we would have been in really big trouble.'

'Aha!' replied Mr Bold, brightening up instantly. 'I tracked you! We hyenas have an excellent sense of smell, remember? I picked up your scent by the back door and just followed it all the way to the school. Had to keep pretending I'd dropped something as passers-by wondered why I was sniffing the pavement.'

Back at 41 Fairfield Road, Annika was delighted with the bin full of ants.

'Delicious!' she declared, her long tongue lapping up mouthfuls of the juicy insects hungrily. 'This is a proper meal. Thank you so much. This should keep me going until suppertime at least!'

Bobby, Betty and Minnie looked at each other and laughed.

Before we get on to the next chapter, might I just refer you back to the beginning of this book and my ruminations on right and wrong . . . remember?

Do you think the twins were right or wrong to break in to the school to get some ants for their hungry visitor? Were they being kind or were they being naughty? Perhaps you and your friends can have a heated debate about it. That'll pass the time.

Chapter 10

As you know, the Bolds were in the midst of clearing out the spare bedroom for Fifi the poodle. So Mrs Bold was wondering how and where they were going to accommodate Annika, when the aardvark herself came up with a solution. Soon after polishing off her bin full of ants, she began to yawn.

'Do you mind, Amelia, if I take a nap now?'

'Of course,' replied Mrs Bold. 'You must be very tired after sleeping in the streets without a proper bed.'

'Yes, although a proper bed doesn't suit me. Aardvarks sleep in burrows in the wild . . . I actually have my eye on your cupboard under the stairs. Might I slip in there, do you think?'

'No problem, Annika,' replied Mrs Bold, moving to the hall and opening the cupboard door. 'I'll just move the hoover and the ironing board out the way for you.'

'I won't need much space. We sleep curled up in a ball. That laundry basket would be ideal.' And Annika slipped past Mrs Bold and into the basket. 'Lovely!' she said with a contented sigh.

'Sure it won't be too dark or dusty in here?'

But Annika was already asleep, snoring contentedly as soon as her eyes were closed. Mr Bold came to see that their guest was comfortable.

'Sleeping like a baby,' said Mrs Bold, in hushed tones.

What do baby footballers do in their sleep?

Dribble!

Mrs Bold closed the cupboard door so her laughing didn't disturb Annika.

The next day everyone continued getting the spare room ready for Fifi. Mr Bold and Uncle Tony said they'd do the decorating. Miranda the monkey would do the hard-to-reach spots.

'Fifi is a big star these days. It won't do as it is,' said Mr McNumpty. 'She's used to luxury!'

'Smells a bit too,' pointed out Uncle Tony.

'That's hardly surprising,' agreed Mr McNumpty. 'There's been all manner of guests in there. I can smell fox, otter and goose – and we haven't even got to the top of the stairs yet!'

'What colour shall we paint it?' asked Tony.

'Yellow, I think,' said his friend decisively. 'Buttercup yellow. Nice and cheerful. It'll go beautifully with the orange pattern in the carpet.'

'Er, that's not a pattern,' pointed out Uncle Tony. 'It's a stain left by Craig the wild boar. He didn't always make it to the loo on time.'

But eventually the decorating was done and the carpet, curtains and windows were cleaned. Everyone worked very hard to make the room perfect. A new mattress for the bed was needed as the old one was beyond saving (Craig, again – but let's not dwell on his personal hygiene issues. Boars will be boars, is all I can say). A new dressing table was acquired for nothing from a FreeCycle website, together with a smart new chair.

Finally Mrs Bold placed a lovely vase of flowers on the windowsill.

'Well done, everyone!' she declared.

The following Saturday the Bolds, together with Mr McNumpty and Uncle Tony, were having a soya mince shepherd's pie for their lunch. Annika was snoozing in her laundry basket in the cupboard under the stairs and Mr Bold was amusing everyone with some jokes as usual:

Suddenly they heard a car horn beep. Everyone rushed to the front door to see a large shiny limousine with blacked-out windows parked outside.

'She's here!' cried Mrs Bold. 'Fifi's here at last!'

The driver, looking very smart and wearing a peaked cap, got out of the car and strode round to open the back door and help the passenger out. Wearing dark glasses, a veil and a floor-length faux fur coat, Fifi emerged. She raised a gloved hand to cover her face.

'*S'il vous plaît!*' she said in her thick French accent. 'No photos, please!' and she swept up the garden.

'Gosh,' murmured Betty.

'Isn't she beautiful!' said Mrs Bold, wiping a tear from her eye. 'Welcome home, Fifi dearest!'

Fifi greeted everyone with a kiss on each cheek. '*Merci! Merci!*' Then Mr Bold helped the chauffeur carry in her matching set of twelve Louis Vuitton suitcases.

Finally everyone settled in the lounge and tea was served. Fifi sat on the sofa, Bobby and Betty either side of her, and removed her dark glasses and veil.

'Ah, it is good to be back,' she said, hugging the twins affectionately. 'You all look so well!'

'How have you been, old girl?' asked Mr McNumpty.

'*Old*?' repeated Fifi.

'I mean – no, not old – young! Er, how has it all been going?'

'My voice is better than ever. I am a huge success,' said Fifi modestly. 'It is a gift.' She shrugged. 'But I never forget my humble roots, *ici* in Teddington.'

'No place like home, eh?' said Mr Bold.

'*Ce'st vrai*,' nodded Fifi, pausing to reapply her Russian Red lipstick. 'I owe all of my success to you Bolds. All of you.'

'We're so pleased for you,' said Mrs Bold. 'Really we are.'

'And I have missed you,' she continued. 'You understand me better than anyone else. And do you know what I would really like? What I crave?'

'Caviar?' asked Mrs Bold, looking slightly worried.

'Champagne?' offered Uncle Tony.

'Non!' Fifi lowered her voice. 'What I want – what I 'ave been dreaming of – is a big, juicy bone!'

What did the French skeleton call his friend?

Bone ami!

'There's a nice bone in the fridge,' said Mrs Bold when the laughing stopped. 'Run and get it, would you, Bobby?'

'Yes, sir-ee!' said Bobby.

Fifi began to salivate at the prospect, causing her lipstick to bubble a bit at the corners of her mouth. 'I'd better remove my manteau,' she said excitedly, taking off her coat. 'Et mes gloves!'

Bobby returned carrying a large bone and Fifi got down on the floor, held the bone between her front paws and began to gnaw on it hungrily. 'Mmmm, c'est delicious!' she said contentedly.

Everyone sat and watched Fifi make quick work of her treat.

Mrs Bold observed that without her coat on, their former pupil had put on a bit of weight. But knowing how sensitive showbiz people are about such things she decided it was probably best not to say anything. The meal portions on cruise ships were known to be generous and who could blame Fifi for enjoying the first-class catering?

When the bone was finished, Fifi licked her lips and sat back down on the sofa, allowing herself a rather unladylike burp.

'Ah! That was *merveilleuse!*' she declared. 'It hit the spot perfectly!'

Then there was a scratching sound at the door and it swung open to reveal Annika, dressed in a floral winceyette nightie and yawning.

'Eek!' shrieked Fifi. '*Qui est-ce?*'

'Come on in, Annika,' said Mrs Bold. 'Meet Fifi.' Annika smiled at Fifi and gave her a sniff with her long snout.

'Pleased to meet you. Everyone has been very excited waiting for your visit.'

Fifi wagged her tail and sniffed the aardvark in return, from head to toe.

'Nice to meet you,' she said. 'Je suis Fifi Lampadaire, singer extraordinaire.'

'French poodle, unless I'm mistaken? Happy to make your acquaintance.'

'*Oui,*' confirmed Fifi. 'Likewise.'

'Fifi?' asked Bobby. 'Your postcard said you had a "little problem". We've been wondering what it is.'

'Are you OK?' added Betty.

Everyone looked expectantly at Fifi.

'Ah, *oui,*' she said, looking a little serious.

'Nothing bad, I hope?' asked Mrs Bold.

'Whatever the problem, we Bolds can sort it out,' said Mr Bold cheerfully.

'*Merci*,' said Fifi. 'Perhaps "problem" was the wrong word to use. But it is the reason I 'ad to leave the cruise ship. The reason I wanted to come 'ome.' She patted her tummy gently. 'Did I mention my adorable Samir in my postcard?'

'You did,' said Betty. '"Très romantique!", you said.'

Fifi nodded. 'Yes, indeed. We are in love!'

'Ahhh!' said Mrs Bold. 'That's lovely. I'm so happy for you.'

'*Merci*. Samir is part of the onboard security service on the ship.'

'A police dog?' asked Mr Bold.

'Oui. He is so brave, mon Samir. And handsome . . .'

What do you call a dog detective?

Sherlock Bones!

'But why does that mean you had to leave the ship?' asked Mr McNumpty reasonably.

Fifi gazed at the mantelpiece for a moment. 'Well, sometimes when two people are in love, then a happy event happens . . .'

There was a thoughtful silence in the room, broken by a gasp from Mrs Bold.

'Oh. Oh! OH! You're pregnant!' Mrs Bold jumped up and hugged Fifi.

'Merci,' said Fifi. '*Oui*. My pups are due any day!'

'That explains fat 𝐭𝐮𝐦-𝐭𝐮𝐦!' squeaked Miranda from the top of the curtain rail.

'𝐂𝐨𝐧𝐠𝐫𝐚𝐭𝐮𝐥𝐚𝐭𝐢𝐨𝐧𝐬, Fifi dearest,' said Mrs Bold, clasping her paws together with delight. 'What 𝐡𝐚𝐩𝐩𝐲 news!'

'We're going to have puppies to play with!' exclaimed Betty.

'And clear up after . . .' added Uncle Tony.

'𝐏𝐨𝐨𝐩𝐢𝐞-𝐬𝐜𝐨𝐨𝐩𝐢𝐞,' squeaked Miranda.

Fifi yawned. 'But now, *je suis si fatigué.* Please could you show me to my room? Walking on my hind legs in my condition isn't easy.'

The twins led Fifi upstairs and proudly showed her the newly decorated yellow bedroom.

'*C'est magnifique!*' declared the poodle, settling herself on the comfy bed. 'Would you draw the curtains for me? I think I need to rest.'

'Shall we see you in the morning?' asked Bobby.

'*Oui, mes chéries*. Maybe a tray with some warm milk and another delicious bone? Goodnight!'

The twins closed the door behind them and left Fifi to sleep.

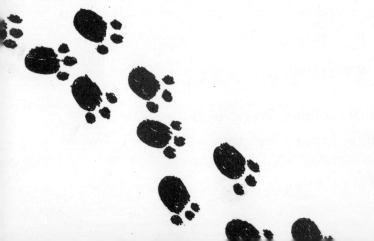

Chapter

While Fifi rested in the spare room, Bobby, Betty and Minnie's time was fully occupied in the endless search for enough ants to keep Annika's voracious appetite at bay. They couldn't risk breaking in to the school again, that was for sure. And they didn't really need to. Ants are everywhere, as you may have noticed, but to find a meal's worth, the nest had to be located.

'All we have to do is find an ant, then follow it until it goes home. Then bingo, that's where the nest will be, surely?' said Minnie.

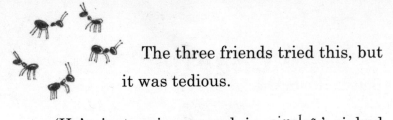

The three friends tried this, but it was tedious.

'He's just going round in circles,' sighed Bobby, after watching an ant in the garden for more than ten minutes. 'There must be a better way. I'm going cross-eyed!'

'And I've been following my ant for ages too,' complained Betty. 'This way, that way, ziggy-zaggy all over the path, then he disappeared into a crevice, never to be seen again. I'm bored. Why can't Annika just eat a sandwich? That would be much simpler. Humph!'

'We mustn't give up,' said Minnie, who was more patient than the hyena twins. 'And if Annika ate a sandwich, it wouldn't agree with her and she would get ill. We don't want that, do we?'

'I suppose not,' said Bobby grudgingly.

'Well, if you're so clever, you find the nest,' said Betty, crossing her arms. 'I'm done with this.'

'OK,' agreed Minnie. 'Ants live in colonies. And just like us, they have to keep their homes clean. We need to look for little mounds of earth or wood shavings. This is their refuse.'

'Like a rubbish tip?' asked Bobby.

'*Exactly,*' nodded Minnie. 'The ants will be close by, I'm sure of it.'

'I've seen some little *pyramids* just like that at the end of the garden!' cried Betty.

'Eureka!' said Minnie excitedly. 'Show me.'

Betty led the way to the end of the path next to the shed and, sure enough, there were several mounds of what looked like finely sieved earth and sawdust. And lots of ants nearby, busily going about their ant business.

'Yes!' said Minnie. 'Well done, Betty. You see, there is always a solution to any problem if you think about it in a logical way. Now we just need to get a half-chewed toffee and a container – maybe not the bin this time – like before, and the ants will march inside it!'

'I've got a better idea,' said Bobby, who didn't like the idea of wasting a toffee every time Annika was peckish.

'What is it?' asked Minnie.

'Well, Annika doesn't need breakfast in bed like Fifi, does she? *She's* not expecting babies. Why don't we bring Annika to the nest and she can help herself?'

'Brilliant!' said Minnie. 'Wish I'd thought of that!'

So they went back to the house and tapped on the door to the cupboard under the stairs.

'Ye-es?' said a tired-sounding Annika. 'Who is it?'

Bobby opened the cupboard door. 'We've found some fresh ants for you. Would you like to come and get them?'

Annika jumped out of her laundry basket, put on her dressing gown, then rubbed her eyes and licked her lips at the same time.

'Ooh, lovely! Let me at them!'

No sooner had they gone through the back door than Annika's nose began to twitch.

'Over here,' she stated, pointing in the direction of the ants and marching confidently down the garden path.

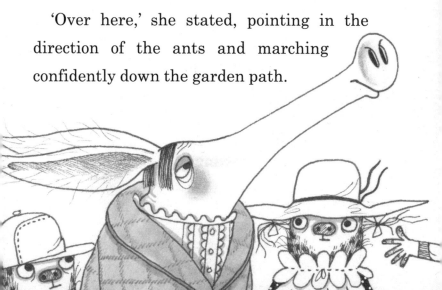

'You've got an even better sense of smell than us!' laughed Betty.

'I have when it comes to ants,' agreed Annika. 'In fact, I can tell you now there are several more colonies in this garden and next door.' She stopped and inhaled, her eyes momentarily closed. 'Seven, eight . . . there are ten or more within a few metres of where I'm standing now.'

'Gosh,' said Betty, impressed.

'So, really, we don't need to find ants for you all the time?' asked Minnie.

'No, dear. I'm quite self-sufficient. Now if you'll excuse me?'

The twins and Minnie watched as she then glided purposefully towards the garden shed, tripping over her dressing gown a couple of times as she went. Once Annika located the nest, she lowered her head and began licking up the ants, humming quietly with delight.

'Happy aardvark!' declared Minnie.

'And happy us,' said Minnie. 'Now we don't have to spend all day looking for ants, we can go and play! If only we'd thought of that earlier.'

But what was to become of Annika? Was she just going to go on living under the stairs for ever? Mr and Mrs Bold wondered about this, and thought they should try to find out what exactly their visitor's hopes and expectations might be. She was no trouble – cucumbers weren't expensive, and in fact they'd started to grow some in the vegetable patch, while ants, of course, were everywhere. No, it wasn't that they wanted Annika to move on, but they sensed, somehow, that 41 Fairfield Road wasn't her ultimate life destination.

The next morning after breakfast, Mr Bold turned the conversation to Annika's future plans.

'I'm glad you brought it up,' said Annika. 'When I escaped from the zoo with Charlie and Fergie, our main objective was freedom. To get away from there and find you. We didn't have any plans about what to do after that. We all just wanted to stick together. But then, once I was free, Fergie went to get Charlie and, as I told you, she never returned.'

'You must worry about your friends,' said Mrs Bold.

'Poor Aardy-varky,' called Miranda from the top of the kitchen cupboard.

'Maybe Fergie forgot where she'd dropped me? Or she got spooked by the searchlight? Or they're still trapped in there,' said Annika with despair.

'Maybe they escaped and Fergie has attempted to fly back to Australia,' suggested Mr Bold.

'I doubt it. It's too far, especially with her weak wing,' pointed out Annika. 'I thought they might come here. That we could all meet up as planned. But it has been a week now, and there has been no sign.'

'You'd think someone would notice a skunk in the vicinity!' joked Mr Bold.

'Stinky-stinky!' squealed Miranda.

'Yes, quite,' agreed Annika. 'Charlie can be quite **pungent** if he's in the mood.'

How many skunks does it take to make a big stink?

Quite a PHEW!

What do you call a flying skunk?

A smell-icopter!

'That's rather good,' commented Annika, joining in with the laughter. 'Any more skunk jokes?'

'Er . . .' said Mr Bold. 'Of course!'

> Why didn't the skunk call his parents?

> Because his phone was out of odour!

Mr McNumpty suddenly stood up. 'Wait a minute. Those skunk jokes have reminded me of an article in yesterday's paper, concerning a terrible smell.'

'Really?' said Mr Bold.

'Yes. Where is yesterday's newspaper?'

'In the garage in the recycling bin,' Mr Bold replied.

'Could you get it for me?'

Mr Bold went off to dig it out.

'Something to do with my missing friends?' asked Annika, frowning. 'In the paper?'

'I'm not sure,' mumbled Mr McNumpty. 'It might be nothing, but worth checking out, perhaps. Didn't think much about it at the time. But now . . .'

Mr Bold rushed in, carrying a rather screwed-up newspaper. 'This one?' he asked.

'Yes.' Mr McNumpty began scanning each page quickly before turning to the next. Eventually he stopped and pointed to a photograph of Big Ben.

'Aha!' he said. 'Listen to this. It's only a short article on page eight, but interesting, I think.' And he began to read. 'Climate change Activists Try to Turn Back Time is the headline.' Then he continued reading aloud.

Two climate change activists who scaled the side of Big Ben caused the historic clock at Westminster Palace to be stopped yesterday for safety reasons. The pair, thought to be from the large encampment who have been living in tents in Parliament Square for several weeks, began their ascent shortly before 5 p.m. yesterday afternoon. The famous bongs were stopped for safety reasons during the demonstration. Once they reached the clock face they unfurled a homemade banner which read 'MAKE OUR PLANET GREEN AGAIN!' Both protestors were arrested shortly afterwards.

'Good on them!' said Annika. 'In sub-Saharan Africa, we aardvarks need grass and woodlands to live in. There is far too much concrete around, in my opinion.'

'Shame for the tourists, though, who'd travelled all the way to London to hear Big Ben's famous chimes,' said Uncle Tony, shaking his head sadly.

'But listen to the last paragraph,' said Mr McNumpty. 'What do you make of this?'

Climate protestors were also thought to be responsible for setting off a stink bomb in the public gallery of Westminster Palace, which caused the House of Commons to be evacuated during Prime Minister's Questions yesterday. One MP suggested the smell was skunk-like.

Annika gasped. 'Stink bomb? Skunk-like? That's Charlie, surely?!' she cried.

'Seems too much to just be a coincidence, doesn't it?' said Mr McNumpty, passing the newspaper to Bobby and Betty.

'Yes,' agreed Mr Bold. 'I think you might be onto something here.'

'Wait a minute,' interrupted Bobby excitedly. 'Look at the photo. Can you see what I can see?'

Everyone peered over his shoulder at the newspaper and the photo of Big Ben and the Houses of Parliament.

'Nice banner,' commented Mrs Bold approvingly.

'Waste of a sheet, if you ask me,' said Uncle Tony.

What did the watch say to the clock?

Hour you doing!

'No, no, no!' said Betty crossly. 'You're not looking properly. Bobby's right. There, under that turret, above the clockface. To the left, slightly.' Her hairy paw directed their attention to a small, dark blob. 'See it?'

Everyone peered closer. Uncle Tony put his reading glasses on.

'Just a SHADOW, isn't it?' said Mrs Bold.

'Maybe, maybe not,' said Bobby. 'But I think it might be something else.'

'What exactly?' said Mr Bold, squinting at the photo intensely.

Suddenly Annika began to breathe faster. 'Ah! I – I think I see something!'

Betty smiled and nodded. 'See the way it's ʜaɴɢɪɴɢ there, the shadow? And look at the outline. Turn it upside down. Now half close your eyes.'

'It's just like a rather large bɑ†!' said Annika. 'Could it really be Fergie?'

'Well, I never. I think it might be,' agreed Mrs Bold.

'Why, I do believe you're right, kids!' said Uncle Tony, giving the twins an affectionate pat on the back.

'Well spotted,' said Mr Bold.

The group sat back down at the table and looked at each other, eyes shining with excitement.

'But why would Fergie the fruit bat and Charlie the skunk be living in the Palace of Westminster?' wondered Annika, scratching her head. 'Did they get lost?'

'And what do we do now?' asked Uncle Tony.

'This possible sighting and the alleged stink bomb both need investigating,' summed up Mr McNumpty.

'Well, I think this calls for a family trip to Westminster, don't you?' said Mrs Bold. 'Children, go and get ready. And I'd better check on Fifi before we leave.'

Chapter

While the twins were getting themselves ready for the expedition to Westminster, Mrs Bold tapped gently on Fifi's bedroom door and entered with some breakfast. But Fifi was panting a little and asked for the curtains to remain closed.

'I wish to be alone, Amelia. Do not disturb me, *s'il vous plaît*.'

'Are you all right, Fifi?' asked Mrs Bold.

'I think,' said Fifi, between pants, 'that my puppies are on their way.'

'Do you need anything?' asked Mrs Bold in a state of nervous excitment. 'Hot water? Towels?'

'No need, Amelia. I think I will be fine.'

Mrs Bold went downstairs to tell everyone the wonderful news and they all agreed that they couldn't go to Westminster now and leave Fifi alone. Besides, the twins were far too excited to see the puppies. They didn't want to miss their arrival. So for the next few hours, the Bolds were careful not to make too much noise. The only exception was when Annika knocked over a vase accidentally and there was a bit of a clatter.

It was early afternoon when Mrs Bold heard some high-pitched little yelps coming from Fifi's room, so she went upstairs with the twins following close behind, and gently knocked on the door. 'Hello, Fifi?'

'Come in!' said Fifi, sounding tired but happy. 'Come and see my babies!'

Mrs Bold and the twins gently opened the door and entered the darkened room. The bed was empty, but then they spotted Fifi, lying inside one of the open Louis Vuitton cases. Nestling next to her were five of the cutest puppies ever seen.

'Meet my shepadoodles,' said Fifi proudly. All five were mainly white with black ears and a few splodges. Their eyes were closed and they wriggled and nuzzled, trembling slightly.

'Oh my, Fifi,' whispered Mrs Bold. 'Aren't they wonderful?'

'My Samir will be so thrilled,' replied Fifi, giving them a gentle lick.

'And are you OK?' asked Mrs Bold.

'I am very well, thank you. Filled with so much happiness,' she said quietly. 'Overcome with love!'

Mrs Bold and the twins stayed for a little, admiring the pups and congratulating their mother, but decided to leave her in peace to bond with her litter and recover from the birth.

'I'll bring you something nice and wholesome to eat a bit later,' said Mrs Bold, as she stood up to leave. 'We're just popping out to, er, visit Big Ben.'

'A good name for one of my pups,' pondered Fifi, as she tucked into the afterbirth.

Chapter

So, a couple of hours later, Mr and Mrs Bold, together with the twins, Mr McNumpty and Annika, emerged from Westminster tube station. (Uncle Tony and Miranda had opted to stay at home as they were rather tired and Fifi might need a drink or a snack.) The group gazed in wonder at the famous Westminster Palace and squinted up at Big Ben, although nothing significant seemed apparent. There were lots of tourists taking photos, and many cars, bicycles, police officers and some police horses too, who gave the Bolds a knowing look.

'What do we do now?' asked Betty.

'Er, I'm not sure yet,' admitted Mr Bold. 'Annika? What do you think?' But Annika was a bit overcome by the crowds and the noise and had pulled her hood up over her head.

'I don't know where to begin, to be honest,' she said, her voice a little shaky. 'This may all be a mistake. How did we ever expect to spot them here?'

They wandered over Westminster Bridge and back again and then peered inside the grand doors of Westminster Abbey. Every now and then Mr McNumpty got his binoculars out and scanned the horizon, paying particular attention to the top of Big Ben. But there was no sight of anything bat-shaped and no smell of skunk. Annika shook her head and sighed.

'Let's cross over to the green,' suggested Betty. 'I'd like to see the statues while we're here.'

'Good idea,' said Mrs Bold. 'There's a bronze of Winston Churchill over there.' She lowered her voice. 'I've heard rumours he was a bulldog, you know.'

They ambled around Parliament Square. There were lots of tents with colourful flags and bunting where climate change campaigners were camping out. Betty admired their mohair jumpers and baggy cheesecloth trousers.

'They're all smiling and look so friendly!' she declared.

A girl with braided hair even offered her a biscuit. 'Try a vegan surprise?' she said. 'Made from sustainably farmed buckwheat.'

Betty accepted and declared it to be delicious, if a bit chewy.

Eventually they all grew tired and sat down on the grass.

'It's hard to know where to begin, isn't it?' said Annika. 'I had no idea it would be so busy!'

'Yes, dear,' said Mrs Bold. 'But it was worth a try. Why not take your hood off? If Fergie or Charlie *are* here, we need them to spot you.'

'But people might stare at me,' replied Annika. 'I'm very self-conscious about my long nose.'

'Oh, I wouldn't worry about that,' said Mr McNumpty. 'They have all sorts here.'

So Annika pulled her hood down and looked around hopefully. But nothing happened.

'It'll be dark soon,' said Bobby gloomily. 'Perhaps it was a silly idea of mine. What we thought was a bat might have been a trick of the light.'

190

'Shall we just go home then?' asked Betty despondently.

'Soon,' said Mrs Bold. 'But we're here now so let's just wait a little longer, shall we?'

'Oh, look over there,' said Betty. 'That's the statue of Millicent Fawcett, the women's suffragette campaigner.'

She went for a closer inspection.

'I like her banner,' she said, reading it aloud: 'COURAGE CALLS TO COURAGE EVERYWHERE.'

'Yes, I like it too!' said Mrs Bold. 'Fred? Nigel? We must not give up. Like the suffragettes, who fought for human women to have the vote, we must be courageous, do you hear?'

'Quite right,' said Mr McNumpty, suddenly looking energised and standing up. 'Our two missing animal chums might be here somewhere and we must work harder to find them!'

'I do believe they *are* here,' said Annika, sniffing the air. 'I can just sense it!'

'Courage!' cried Betty.

'Where are they, though? They could be anywhere . . .' said Bobby. 'It's like looking for a needle in a haystack!'

Suddenly Mr Bold jumped in the air.

'Aha!' he said excitedly. 'You've given me an idea, Bobby!'

'Have I?' said Bobby. 'How?'

'Hay,' said Mr Bold. 'Haystack. Who eats hay? Horses! What horses are there round here? Police horses!'

'Yee-ees?' nodded Bobby, looking confused.

'Well, if anyone knows where to find a skunk and a fruit bat, it will be a fellow animal, won't it? The horses might know if they are here or not, they're on duty every day, and if Charlie and Fergie are here, the horses can tell us where! They clocked us when we arrived, I saw it on their faces.'

'Brilliant idea, Fred!' said Mrs Bold. 'Go and ask them.'

There were two shiny chestnut-brown horses a few metres away, with mounted police officers sitting on their backs scanning the crowds. As the others watched, Mr Bold wandered casually over to the handsome steeds, then stopped close by. He sat nonchalantly on the grass. The others could see him whisper and the horses' heads turning slowly in his direction. A conversation took place, equine lips moving busily while Mr Bold paid careful attention. Eventually the hyena stood up, gave a surreptitious nod of thanks, and walked back to his family, looking as if he might burst with excitement.

'Bingo!' he said.

'Really? They knew something?' asked Annika.

'They certainly did,' said Mr Bold. 'Bobby was right. Fergie is roosting up at the top of Big Ben, here to keep an eye on Charlie.'

'And where is Charlie?' asked Mrs Bold.

'The red tent with the "There Is No Planet B, Folks!" on top, apparently. Pitched in the middle of the square. He's hiding inside with some climate change and animal liberation campaigners called Twig and Swig.'

Chapter 14

Before we meet Twig and Swig, I need to
explain a few things about them. They were
a rather unusual couple. Kind and caring –
they must be, as they'd been looking after a
lost skunk – but there's more. Twig and Swig
had dedicated their whole lives to saving our
planet. They decided ages ago, that if they
wanted the world to be a better, greener,
healthier place, then they had to live up
to their own hopes and expectations. They
travelled around by foot or bicycle and lived
in a tent all year round. Twig and Swig ate
a strictly plant-based vegan diet, refusing all

meat, fish, poultry, eggs and cheese. Instead they enjoyed delicious wholegrains, beans, legumes, tofu, nuts and seeds. They also took care to avoid any animal-derived clothing or accessories, so no leather, wool or fur. All their garments were made from cruelty-free, recycled and sustainable materials. It was all ethical and eco-friendly: footwear was made from recycled rubber, clothing was 100 per cent organic cotton or hemp or Eco-fi, a high-quality fibre created from post-consumer recycled plastic bottles.

And there's more . . . Twig and Swig didn't wish to be identified as male or female. They were what is known as gender fluid − they wanted to remain flexible about whether they were Arthur or Martha, depending on how they felt. So, out of respect, this means I shall not write about 'him' or 'her' or 'she' or 'he'. We must respectfully refer to 'them'

or 'they'. All clear? (I can tell you that Twig has a beard and Swig has a high-pitched voice and wears vegan lipstick, but please don't jump to any conclusions based on that snippet of information. They are non-binary gender variants, and that's all you need to know.) Just remember they were kind and caring and they wouldn't harm a fly. And if they did, it would be an accident and they'd feel very sorry and apologise.

Twig and Swig spent their time moving from one part of the country to another, depending on where they thought their presence was required. They believed that non-violent protests are a necessary means to an end. Sometimes they got arrested, appeared in court and were fined, but they didn't mind this. If they *must* break the law to save the world, then so be it. Once they camped outside at a fracking site near Blackpool, where they lay down in the road to stop the lorries passing. And as members of Plastic Attack UK, they often pushed trolleys filled with unwanted packaging collected from customers outside supermarkets back through the retailers' doors.

Twig and Swig were also keen animal liberationists and no strangers to direct action. In fact, this is how they came to meet Charlie and Fergie. Together with some other animal freedom fighters, they were hiding in woods outside Shorthop Zoo, planning to break in and liberate some inmates, when they were disturbed in the middle of the night by Fergie crash-landing into the side of their tent. The fruit bat, unbalanced by her cargo of skunk, had flown off course. Instead of arriving at the spot where Annika was waiting, Fergie had lost all sense of direction. In the darkness, she panicked and had no idea where she was.

Twig and Swig didn't hesitate to shelter the pair inside their tent, and, guessing they had escaped from the zoo, kept them safe and hidden, and fed them with plenty of nutritious lentil and wild nettle soup.

Fergie and Charlie were impressed by their earnest new friends and, being animals, instinctively knew they were good, kind people. Listening to the humans talk, they understood their heartfelt desire to help save the planet and live blameless carbon-free lives.

When Twig and Swig decided they were going off to London to join a major global warming protest, the fruit bat and the skunk were taken along with them. They settled themselves in the red tent in Parliament Square – cramped but safe, and enjoyed the adventure. Of course they worried about their lost companion, Annika, and hoped, eventually, to find their way to Teddington.

Fergie found the group's habit of folk singing and improvised drumming a trifle wearing (she remembered the Aboriginals' music from Australia and thought they did it much better), so in the evenings she would fly off to roost at the top of Big Ben, where it was more peaceful, apart from the chimes.

It was Swig's idea to hide Charlie inside their anorak and smuggle him into the public gallery of the Houses of Parliament. The stink bomber was really Charlie the skunk, of course, making his feelings clear about the current government's paltry efforts to lower carbon emissions!

The Bolds' party soon located the bright red tent with the 'There Is No Planet B, Folks!' banner. There was no door to knock on, so they loitered expectantly outside the zipped flaps for a moment before Mr Bold cleared his throat and said: 'Er, hello? Could I speak to Twig and Swig, please?' There was a rustling inside the tent and then the zip was lowered a little and a face appeared.

'Twig here,' said a friendly voice. 'Friend or foe?'

'Oh, friend, definitely,' said Mr Bold.

'Ha! Very funny!' smiled Twig, who then unzipped the tent completely and jumped out together with another person.

'How do you do?' they said. 'I'm Twig and this is Swig. How can we help you?' A smell of sweet incense wafted out from the tent.

'We're the Bolds – well, most of us are. And we've brought our friend Annika with us. We hear you might know the whereabouts of her pets, who happen to be a skunk and a fruit bat?'

Annika stepped forward, introduced herself and shook the protestors' hands warmly.

'Pleased to meet you,' said the aardvark.

Twig and Swig looked at each other, somewhat surprised by her appearance.

'Are you the police?' asked Twig.

'Oh, no, no, no, nothing like that I can assure you,' said Mr Bold.

'Although we have done quite bit of detective work to find you!' chipped in Mr McNumpty.

Mr Bold's mention of a skunk and a fruit bat seemed more than a coincidence, but Twig wanted to be sure. They looked at the aardvark. 'Where did you lose your "pets"?'

'Outside Shorthop Zoo,' replied Mr Bold. 'You can trust us.'

Twig and Swig smiled serenely at each other and then at their visitors. They were so kind and so evolved, they knew, at a glance, if someone was honest or not. It was as if they could see into people's hearts and souls. They nodded simultaneously, each knowing what the other was thinking and in agreement.

'You are honest people,' stated Swig. 'We can tell.'

'We can't fit you all inside our tent, but would Annika like to come and speak to her "pets"?'

A moment later Annika was perched on a low stool inside the zipped-up tent with Swig and Twig. Swig then opened up a duffle bag and spoke gently into the opening.

'Are you awake? Someone has come to see you!' There were one or two sleepy snuffling noises and then a glistening black nose appeared, twitching and sniffing, followed by a furry black head with a dramatic white stripe along the crown.

'Charlie!' cried Annika. 'I am so pleased to see you again!'

The skunk's dark eyes opened wide in amazement and he immediately wriggled out of the bag and leaped to the aardvark's side, sniffing and licking with joy.

'My friend, I can't believe it! What happened to you?'

'I waited in the woods outside the zoo for you and Fergie for ages. Then I realised something must have gone wrong and I was on my own. I made my way to Teddington.'

'Ah, the Bolds! Of course!' said Charlie. 'How clever of you. We were very lucky, as it happens. We crash-landed into a campsite of eco-warriors and they looked after us.' Charlie nodded towards Swig and Twig. 'But how did you know I was here?'

'We didn't for sure. But the stink bomb in Parliament? We guessed it was you! And how is Fergie? Is her wing still all right?'

'As good as new, thank you,' came a muffled voice from inside an organic hemp sleeping bag.

'Fergie, you're here too!' said Annika, as the

fruit bat emerged, yawning, then, after a hop and a flap of wings, she hung from the top of the tent roof, smiling down at her long-lost friend.

'Drums, bells, incense,' she muttered. 'This saving-the-world business has given me one of my headaches!'

Half an hour later, Annika emerged from the tent carrying a beaded, synthetic leather, toxic-free and rather full holdall. She gave Twig and Swig a long, heartfelt hug.

'*Namaste*,' said Twig.

'Love and light,' said Swig. 'Go in peace. We hope to see you all again one day.'

Everyone waved and the Bolds' party made their way to the Underground station. The holdall proved a little too heavy for Annika to carry, so Mr McNumpty took over.

'Be careful with it,' said Annika. 'Precious cargo inside.'

Mr McNumpty gave Annika a knowing wink.

Chapter
15

Grateful as they were to Twig and Swig and the other climate change protestors, it was clear that Fergie and Charlie were happy to be moving on. Fergie, with her super-sensitive hearing, had an almost permanent headache from the enthusiastic singing and drumming, not to mention the chimes of Big Ben. And Charlie couldn't spend all his time hidden in tents and duffle bags – he'd get cramp. So everyone was happy when they all got back to 41 Fairfield Road. A big supper was spread out on the kitchen table and Fifi carried her puppies down one by one to a new basket by the radiator. They were trying to climb over each other and tentatively sniffing everyone's feet.

The Bolds were always happiest when the house was full of visitors, and everyone got along splendidly, chatting, asking questions, playing with the pups and laughing at Mr Bold's jokes.

It had been a busy day, and eventually Mr McNumpty and Uncle Tony said goodnight, the twins went upstairs for their bath, Annika headed to her cupboard under the stairs and Fifi curled up in the basket with her five contented puppies.

'I'll clear the table,' said Mr Bold. 'Which reminds me—'

Where does the Devil do his washing-up?

In Helsinki!

'Let me think,' said Mrs Bold. 'Where will Fergie and Charlie sleep?'

'No bed needed for a fruit bat,' said Fergie

cheerfully. 'I'll just hang upside down from the curtain rail. Without Big Ben chiming every fifteen minutes, it will be bliss!'

'As for me,' said Charlie, 'I'd be quite content to slip into the basket with Fifi and the pups. Nice and cosy.'

Fifi raised her head and glared at the skunk with her lip curled. 'Certainement not!' she spat. 'That is une suggestion inappropriate! I am not sharing my bed with a skunk!'

'Er, I think I'll make you up a bed in the lounge, Charlie,' said Mrs Bold hurriedly.

'And lock the door!' muttered a horrified Fifi.

An hour later the washing-up had all been done, 41 Fairfield Road was in darkness and everyone was sleeping soundly. Everyone except Fifi, that is. As a mum to hungry pups, she woke every few hours to feed and groom her litter. It was just before four in the morning when she heard a scratching at the back door and a gentle whimpering sound. She listened attentively for a moment and then her heart began to race.

'Oh, *mon dieu!*' she said and got out of the basket. 'Un moment, *s'il vous plaît!*' she said. She quickly licked her lips and fluffed up her ears with her paw, then unlocked the back door.

'*Ma chérie*, it's you!' she cried, as a handsome, dark-furred German shepherd leaped into the room, tail wagging furiously, kissing her all over.

'Samir! Is it really you?'

'It is me, your Samir, of course! I could not stay away, my darling.'

Fifi led Samir to the basket. 'And look. You are a father. Meet our beautiful children.' Awoken by the disturbance, the puppies all squeaked excitedly at their father, their little tails quivering.

'Ah, they are perfect. Five pups! I am so proud!' said Samir, shaking his head, then gently sniffing and licking each one.

He turned to Fifi and gazed lovingly at her. 'You have made me the happiest dog in the world.'

'But 'owever did you get 'ere?' asked Fifi.

'A stroke of good luck, dearest. My handler has been posted to London on a special, top-secret mission,' said Samir. 'We are staying at the Embassy in Belgravia. Our kennels are guarded by an old friend of mine. He let me out but I had to promise to return before daylight. I just had to see you.'

'You cannot stay?' wailed Fifi, crestfallen.

Samir shook his head. 'No, I can't. But to see you again and meet the pups – however briefly – is better than nothing. We must be happy.'

'Always,' said Fifi, snuggling into Samir's luxurious dark mane of fur and closing her eyes. 'These few moments with you will last me a lifetime.'

'I must go,' said Samir. 'I will come and see you again when I can get away.'

'*Je t'adore* for ever,' whispered Fifi.

A few minutes later, Samir left.

In the morning Fifi tearfully told Mrs Bold all about her romantic night-time visitation.

'How lovely, dear!' said Mrs Bold, sweeping the tufts of dark German shepherd fur from the kitchen floor. 'Looks as if Samir is moulting too. This is just what I'm looking for to decorate the brim of my latest hat.' She picked up the small ball of fur and placed it on the windowsill. 'I do hope he comes again soon. I'm not sure I have enough here.'

'He hopes to,' said Fergie helpfully, from the curtain rail. With her excellent hearing she had heard the whole conversation. 'If he can get away from his duties at the Embassy. My fur is a bit more gingery than Samir's, but if you'd like to give me a comb, I'm sure it will mix in rather well?'

'Excellent!' declared Mrs Bold. 'Thank you, Fergie. A little touch of ginger never did anyone any harm.'

Chapter 16

The next few weeks passed very pleasantly, and everyone rubbed along together well. The twins were back at school, enjoying their roles as Green Monitors. They raced home every night to see Fifi's puppies, who were growing fast and becoming more adventurous by the day. Samir made several more night-time visits and was suitably proud of their progress. If it was a dry day, Fifi allowed them to play rough and tumble in the garden. Several holes were dug in the lawn. Fortunately Mr Bold wasn't as fussy as Mr Bingham at Number 10, so he didn't mind – he was no stranger to digging himself, of course. As it happened, the digging unearthed several ant colonies, which was very handy for Annika.

Charlie liked to go out and about on a lead with Mr McNumpty and Uncle Tony. People would stare at him with his unusual stripes and give him a stroke, but he only let off his pungent scent once when an old lady accidentally trod on his tail as they crossed Teddington Broad Street. She almost fainted from the smell, but Uncle Tony apologised and blamed it on his 'trouble downstairs' and they moved swiftly on.

Fergie took long flights during the night, stretching her wings and finding fruit and flowers to feast on. She discovered a fine selection of bedding plants at Number 10 Fairfield Road, which she devoured. The Binghams weren't best pleased when they discovered their crop had gone. They were a particularly anxious couple who did not like wildlife of any kind and Mr Bingham blamed the birds and took to throwing stones at them.

Unfortunately Mr and Mrs Bingham were also still very distressed about seeing a young boy urinating in their garden a few weeks ago. They had been keeping a close eye out for the culprit and one day they recognised Bobby Bold going into Number 41.

'Oh, I should have known,' said Mrs Bingham to her husband. 'It was that awful Bolds boy. I don't know why I didn't think of that before. They're a dreadful family and they really let the side down. There's always so much noise and mess coming from their house. And they never stop laughing. I can't stand people who laugh.'

'I've a good mind to go and speak to the boy's parents,' said Mr Bingham. 'The child behaves like an animal. This is a respectable street – not a zoo.'

So one Saturday morning there was a knock at the Bolds' front door. Mrs Bold had just finished clearing away the breakfast things and was rummaging around in her hat-making box for some inspiration. The twins were outside playing with Charlie, and Fifi's puppies were resting in a basket near the stove whilst their mother took a nap upstairs. Mr Bold put down his newspaper and went to answer the knock.

'Ah, Mr Bingham. Good morning.'

'Now listen—' began Mr Bingham crossly.

But Mr Bold interrupted him. 'I'm glad you called. Can I ask you a question?'

'Er, well, yes, I suppose so.'

Why did the rubber chicken cross the road?

To stretch his legs!

Mr Bold laughed loudly at his own joke.

'Mr Bold,' said Mr Bingham. 'This is no laughing matter. I wish to discuss your son's feral behaviour.'

'Oh,' said Mr Bold. 'Then you'd better come inside. He's just playing in the garden.'

Mr Bingham marched right into the kitchen, glancing with disgust at Mrs Bold's new hat. 'Madam, I suggest you recycle your rubbish like the rest of us, rather than wearing it,' he said, rather rudely, sneering at his own joke.

There was a growl from one of Fifi's puppies.

'Ahhhh,' continued Mr Bingham, spying Bobby outside in the garden. 'There's the little scoundrel. I'd like a word with him. His behaviour has been quite shocking.' And he opened the back door and marched out towards the twins, who were teaching Charlie how to catch a ball.

'Come here, young man,' bellowed Mr Bingham so loudly that he made everyone jump. Including Mr McNumpty, who was next door, checking his hives for honey.

'Who? Me?' asked Bobby, clearly rather nervous.

'Yes, you!' snarled Mr Bingham, and he made a grab for the young pup, but tripped over Charlie in the process.

Poor Charlie clearly felt under attack by the neighbour's aggressive manner and was rather anxious for his friend's safety too, so he began to hiss wildly and stamp his feet. Mr Bingham was not a fan of wild animals, having had his garden attacked by a wild boar once, so he instantly backed away.

'What the hell is that?' he demanded. 'That's

not a dog, is it? It's a WIld animal. You can't keep wild animals in Fairfield Road. It should be locked up in a zoo.'

That was the final straw for Charlie. He only used his best weapon in emergencies, but this obviously felt like an emergency. Lifting his tail, he proceeded to squirt the most foul-smelling liquid at a horrified Mr Bingham.

'What the . . . ?' screamed Mr Bingham in alarm. 'Oh my goodness, that is disgusting. That's worse than disgusting, I'm going to be sick!'

To be fair, the smell was particularly awful and the twins quickly went inside out of the way. But the stink continued to drift, over the fence now, to Mr McNumpty, who was just putting the racks back in his beehive. Despite his bee-keeping suit, the smell permeated towards him and when it reached his large nostrils, he too ran into his house in disgust – without putting the beehive back together properly.

Can you imagine what happened next? That's right, those bees made a beeline for Mr Bingham, stinging him vengefully for disturbing their peace with all his screaming.

Opening the back door, he ran through the kitchen of Number 41, down the hall and into the street, with the bees following close behind and the dreadful smell wafting from him.

'Going so soon?' Mr Bold called after him. 'Do come again. But please don't make so much noise next time. Your behaviour has been quite shocking.'

The residents of Number 41 laughed and laughed, and continued their lives in peace once more.

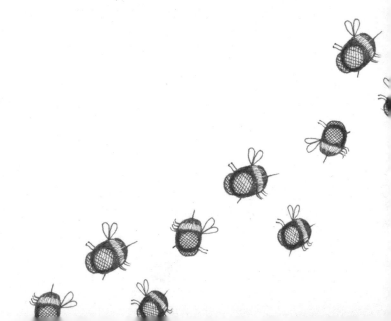

Chapter

17

As time passed cheerily by, one thing became clear: Annika, Charlie and Fergie were friends for ever. Maybe it was their past that bound them together so firmly? They never wanted to go their separate ways and neither did they express any desire to live disguised as humans.

'Sooner or later,' observed Mrs Bold, as she and Mr Bold were strolling through Bushy Park one day, 'I sense they will want to form their own little family.'

'Yes,' said Mr Bold, nodding in agreement. 'But it's difficult to imagine how.'

'Of course, they are welcome to stay with us as long as they wish. I love having them.'

'No trouble at all. Never had such delightful guests.'

'But they're never going to disguise themselves as humans.'

'Or get jobs and earn money,' said Mr Bold.

'So how will it work?' wondered Mrs Bold. 'They can't live on fresh air.'

'The trouble is they aren't naturally wild animals – they've been living in a zoo for too long. But they don't want to live in the human world either, particularly.'

They walked in contemplative silence for a few minutes.

'I know!' said Mr Bold.

'You do?' asked Mrs Bold.

'Well, no, I don't actually know.'

'But you said you did know!'

'I know I did. But I don't.'

'You don't know?'

'No.'

'Now I'm confused!' The hyenas stopped for a long chuckle.

'I'll start again,' said Mr Bold.

'Please do,' said Mrs Bold.

Mr Bold took a deep breath. 'Sometimes you know there is an answer to a problem, but you just don't know what it is yet.'

'The problem?'

'No, the answer!'

'When you don't know what a solution to a problem is, you just need to put it out there. Ask the universe. Then the answer presents itself to you, as if by magic!'

'Oh, I see. How clever.'

'The other day I was hungry. "What am I going to eat?" I wondered. Then I put my hand in my pocket and there was an apple!'

'Amazing!'

'I know,' said Mr Bold. He tilted his head up towards the sky, closed his eyes and raised his voice a little. 'Hello? What is the answer to where our three lovely friends are going to live, please?'

'An aardvark, a skunk and a fruit bat. In Teddington,' said Mrs Bold, filling in some detail for the mysterious, ethereal listener. 'Can you help us? We don't know the answer! How's it going to work, please?'

They opened their eyes, blinked and walked along.

'Nothing has happened,' observed Mrs Bold after a few minutes, sounding disappointed.

'You don't get the answer straight away, silly,' said Mr Bold.

'You got your apple straight away, apparently,' retorted Mrs Bold.

'Ah, that was unusual. Most often you have to wait a while.'

A few moments later, Betty and Bobby came scampering out of the ferns, waving excitedly at their parents.

'Mum! Dad! Guess who we've just met?' called Betty.

'Father Christmas?' suggested Mrs Bold.

Why does Santa always go down the chimney?

Because it soots him!

'No, it was—' Bobby started to explain.

'That's enough, Fred,' said Mrs Bold. 'Bobby is trying to tell us who they met in the ferns.'

But just then the identity of the creature became apparent as a slim, slightly nervous red fox ran up to them and began rubbing her head against Mrs Bold.

'Sylvie!' cried Mrs Bold. 'How lovely to see you!'

Sylvie was a vixen who had lived with the Bolds for some time with her troublesome partner Mossie. (You'll know all about her if you have read *The Bolds in Trouble*, of course.) She now lives happily as a wild fox in Bushy Park, together with Bert, her much nicer fellow fox. (It was a happy ending, which is often the way in the Bolds books, you'll find. But also a true reflection of the author's life experience, as it happens.)

After some affectionate greetings, Mr Bold asked: 'But you are a long way from your den. Don't you live on the other side of the park?'

'We moved,' explained Sylvie. 'An old badger sett became vacant and we fancied a change. Our new home is a few metres away, just over there.'

'How lovely. I'm very happy for you,' said Mrs Bold.

'Thank you,' said Sylvie. 'So lovely to see you all. I'd better be off, though. Bert might wake up and wonder where I've wandered off to.'

'We'll come and see you again soon,' said Betty.

'Er, before you go, Sylvie,' said Mr Bold hurriedly. 'Your old den . . . is it unoccupied?'

'Yes. We only moved a few days ago. Why?' asked Sylvie.

'Well . . . I think we may know of some new

occupants for it.'

'Oh, well, please help yourselves. You know where it is? Under the ancient oak tree, not too far from the park gates near your house.'

'Yes, of course,' said Mr Bold excitedly.

'Bye for now!'

Sylvie disappeared into the ferns again and the Bold family set off in the direction of home.

'Well!' declared Mrs Bold. 'Are you thinking that Annika, Charlie and Fergie might like to live in the old den, dear?'

'I think it might be perfect. What do you think?'

'We'd better go and have a look at it first. But it may be the solution we were looking for.'

'You see?' said Mr Bold. 'Just like I told you!'

'Ask and you shall receive!' said Mrs Bold in wonder. She gave him a squeeze.

The Bolds thought the disused den under the old oak was an ideal residence. The entrance was hidden between some gnarled roots and inside were three fairly large chambers, dry and quiet. It was a bit musty, with a distinct smell of fox, but that couldn't be helped and would surely fade away in time.

'I think it's very cosy,' said Mrs Bold. 'But let's bring Annika, Charlie and Fergie to see for themselves.'

The idea of moving to their own home in Bushy Park thrilled the three house guests.

'That would be amazing!' said Annika. 'We love living with you Bolds, but I like the idea of having our own place – I just couldn't think how we'd ever find one.'

'We'll each have our own room too,' said Charlie. 'And food on our doorstep!'

'I'll probably roost up in the tree,' pointed out Fergie. 'But I'll use my room to store apples there to eat during winter!'

'And we are very nearby,' said Betty. 'We'll

come and visit you and bring you extra fruit if you need it.'

'How wonderful!' said Annika. 'Thank you all so much. I can't wait to see it.'

'We'll go tomorrow,' said Mr Bold. 'Straight after breakfast.'

'I doubt I'll be able to sleep, I'm so excited!' said Annika.

Chapter 18

Sometimes when you're very enthused about something the reality can be a disappointment, don't you find? The Easter egg you've been looking forward to for weeks turns out to be plain chocolate instead of milk and tastes rather bitter. The school trip to Legoland is a washout because it is pouring with rain. The *Britain's Got Talent* final is rubbish because no one has any talent. That sort of thing.

Thus it was when the three prospective tenants went to view their new home.

Mr Bold led the way in and Annika, Charlie and Fergie filed in behind him, followed by Mrs Bold and the twins. There was an awkward silence as Mr Bold switched his torch on and shone it around the earthy walls.

'So, what do you think?' asked Mr Bold.

'Oh,' said Annika flatly. 'I don't want to seem ungrateful, but it's not what I imagined.'

'It's a bit, er, rustic,' said Charlie.

'And it stinks,' added Fergie bluntly.

'I can get you some air freshener,' said Mrs Bold helpfully.

'Thank you,' said Annika, snapping off a root that was dangling from the ceiling.

'There's another chamber through here,' said Bobby, leading the party through a short tunnel.

'Hmmm,' said Fergie, acutely aware of the sound of dripping water.

'It's not quite what we're used to,' said Annika.

'Awfully dark,' said Charlie.

'Oh dear,' said Mr Bold. 'Perhaps we should all go back to Number 41 and have a chat.'

'You don't have to move in here,' said Mrs Bold. 'We thought you'd like it, that's all.'

Annika looked around the den and pulled a face. 'I'm sure it will be lovely when it's finished.'

Back home after a frank conversation, everything became clear: the location and the dimensions of the den were perfect, but the problem was, although they were animals,

246

Annika, Charlie and Fergie were not used to *living* like animals. Years in captivity had domesticated them to a degree, and there was no going back.

'All that earth!' said Fergie. 'So depressing! Couldn't we have carpet on the floor? And wallpaper on the walls?'

'And I'm so used to sleeping in my laundry basket. I don't think I'd be able to just curl up on a pile of old leaves.'

'Oh, I get it,' said Betty. 'You want it to be more homely?'

'That's the word, yes!' nodded Annika. 'You don't think we're being fussy, do you?'

'No, no, I understand,' said Mrs Bold. 'You want what you're used to, that's all.'

'A dark, dirty den seems so primitive,'

explained Charlie with a shudder. 'Even in the zoo we had clean lino floors and dimmed lighting.'

Bobby jumped up suddenly. 'Well, we could make it into a super-den for you!'

Everyone looked very interested in this idea.

'We learned all about it at school, didn't we, Sis?'

'Yes!' said Betty. 'A sustainable, eco-friendly home made entirely from natural materials!'

'A perfect project for Green Monitors!' declared Bobby proudly.

'Yes!' said Annika.

'What fun!' said Mr Bold.

'What clever children!' said Mrs Bold proudly.

Plans were under way the very next day and once Mr McNumpty got wind of it, he declared himself to be Project Manager. The dining room at 39 Fairfield Road became the centre of operations and a sign saying

DEN CONVERSION HQ

was put on the door. There were spreadsheets, diagrams and moodboards sprawled across his mahogany dining table. He even took to keeping a pencil tucked behind his ear, which made him seem very professional.

He gathered everyone together for a briefing.

'Good morning, team. There are a few essential points I wish you to bear in mind at all times. Firstly – secrecy! Remember that this eco-dwelling must be invisible from the outside. However state of the art the interior is to be, to the casual passer-by in Bushy Park it must look like a foxhole. And we must *not* draw attention to ourselves during the construction. We don't want nosy park-keepers asking awkward questions. Understood?'

Everyone nodded.

'Secondly – cost! We have a budget of zero pounds and zero pence at present. I suggest we try and stick to that, so all materials must be recycled or acquired for free.'

Fifi stood up. '*Excusez-moi*. I have une idée . . . I am willing to perform a benefit concert to raise money for the décorations de maison.'

'Oh, Fifi, how kind. That would be wonderful!' said Annika.

'Oui,' agreed Fifi graciously. 'Can someone please book the London Palladium for next Friday?'

'Er, I think it is probably already booked,' said Mrs Bold gently.

'Really?' Fifi tutted. 'Then it will have to be the Albert Hall, je suppose.'

It took another half an hour to convince Fifi that her idea, although very generous, wasn't feasible at such short notice. The fundraising offer looked like it might come to nothing, until Minnie, with careful diplomacy, had a rather brilliant suggestion.

'Do you like Christina Aguilera, Fifi?' she asked.

'*Mais oui.* A little shrill on the high notes, but she is formidable and almost as big a star as moi. *Pourquoi?*'

'It's just that I saw a video on YouTube of her in disguise, busking on the New York subway.'

Fifi's eyes widened in surprise. 'Busking? Non!'

'Yes, it's true. Miley Cyrus does it too.'

'The shame of it!' declared Fifi.

'Not really. I think it shows you are in touch with your fans. Who needs a theatre or a concert hall?'

'Are you suggesting I go and busk on Teddington High Street?'

'Well, why not? Ed Sheeran started out as a busker.'

'Hmmm,' said Fifi. *'Peut-être.* I suppose it might work . . .'

'You'd be a sensation!' said Betty. 'I'll hold the hat for people to put change in.'

'Ten and twenty-pound notes, surely?' corrected Fifi.

'And I'll come and be your bouncer!' offered Bobby.

&-3

So it was that Fifi Lampadaire, singer extraordinaire, was seen howling songs beautifully and accompanying herself on the guitar outside Greggs every afternoon for the next week, her adorable pups sleeping in the guitar case at her feet. Betty, with the help of Miranda, was there to helpfully thrust a hat at passers-by to encourage donations. Lots of money was raised – and several polite enquiries about whether homes were needed for the

pups too.

Merci!

While all this was happening, Mr Bold drove his little blue Honda to the recycling centre where Uncle Tony, Annika and Charlie helped him load it up with everything from old floorboards to water pipes, second-hand insulation, half-used tins of paint, chipboard, a water butt, rolls of discarded wallpaper and even a decorative floral hearth rug.

The twins had never been so busy. It was really quite a project and it took up all their free time. They only wished it wasn't a secret and that they could tell their teacher, Mrs Millin, about it. She'd be so proud of her Green Monitors making an eco-home. It was so much fun all working together, but there was one small thing on Betty's mind.

'Bobby,' she said one morning as they were painting a lovely small chair they'd found. 'Everyone's so busy at the moment, do you think they've forgotten what day it is next week?'

'What day?' he asked.

'You know, the first of May!'

'First of May?' screeched Bobby. 'Really? You mean our birthday? Wow. I'd forgotten myself. I don't know. No one's mentioned it.'

'Mum and Dad are so busy, I feel bad reminding them. And we've got zero pounds and zero pence, remember, so I don't think there's going to be any money for presents.'

'I wish you hadn't reminded me now,' said Bobby. 'Surely they won't forget. It's a big one. We're going to be ten. Double digits.'

But no one seemed to be mentioning it at all. The twins tried to drop hints, like asking Mr Bold what the date would be next Saturday, and asking Mrs Bold for the story of their birth, but Mr Bold was too tired to work it out, and Mrs Bold was too tired to remember. So that seemed to be that.

'Never mind,' said Betty. 'Not many hyenas celebrate their birthday, I'm sure. It's a very human thing to do and we're not really humans.'

Back at HQ Mr McNumpty had calculated the measurements for every wall and floor of the den and materials were cut accordingly then smuggled into the eco-home. Planks of wood were hidden down trouser legs, curtains concealed in backpacks. Bit by bit the new den took shape. A compost loo, a sink and even a camping stove, in case Annika wanted to try some stir-fried ants for a change. Fergie flew back and forth over the park wall in the dead of night, carrying various items, and hid them in the ferns where the twins and Miranda the monkey retrieved them the next day and took them down the foxhole into the den when no one was looking. Guttering was covered in moss to provide a hidden water supply, a concealed ventilation shaft was built too, to provide fresh air, and with Fifi's earnings a few other essential items were purchased: eco-friendly wind-up torches, (second-hand) plates, bowls, pots and pans, a broom, a mop and bucket, bedding, and the all-important laundry basket. Everyone was involved in all aspects of the makeover and the group effort definitely paid off.

Mr McNumpty called everyone into HQ and declared they were just about finished and the new den would be ready for Annika, Charlie and Fergie to move into the next day. The first of May.

'You have worked extremely hard, and I congratulate you all!' he said. 'Project Den is now completed and I'd like to wish the new residents every happiness in their new home. Now let's give ourselves a big round of applause!'

When the clapping and whooping was finished, Annika stood up and wiped a tear from her eye.

'On behalf of Charlie, Fergie and myself, can I thank you all from the bottom of our hearts. The Bolds – and of course I include Mr McNumpty, Uncle Tony, Minnie, Miranda and Fifi – are the loveliest, kindest creatures ever. Not only do you help people – strangers, even – and welcome them into your home, you help them to realise their dreams. We are amazed and for ever grateful to you. You have, quite simply, filled our hearts with happiness and joy – and laughter!'

'Tomorrow we should have a grand opening ceremony,' suggested Mrs Bold.

'A very good idea!' said Fergie.

'Let's all meet at three o'clock by the old oak tree,' said Mr Bold.

'You'll come, won't you, Minnie?' said Mrs Bold.

'I'd love to,' said Minnie.

Mrs Bold gave her a hug. 'It's the twins' birthday tomorrow,' she whispered quietly. 'There will be a cake! And maybe more . . .'

'Oh, thank you!' said Minnie, her eyes shining with delight. 'Betty and Bobby mentioned that it was their birthday. I think they thought you had forgotten, what with all the excitement of building the new den. They didn't like to remind you.'

'Oh no. We haven't forgotten, Minnie dear. Far from it!'

Chapter

In fact, the event in Bushy Park was to be much more than a grand opening for the den. Mr and Mrs Bold wanted to do something lovely for Bobby and Betty's tenth birthday. For weeks they had been secretly planning a surprise party – and as it happened the den completion had occurred at just the right time and provided the perfect cover. Uncle Tony and Mr McNumpty had spent ages secretly making bunting, party food had been bought and hidden, but the best surprise was who was going to be there . . .

As many of the former students and residents of 41 Fairfield Road as possible had been invited. It had been Mr McNumpty's brainwave. 'Let's invite all the animals they know and love,' he'd suggested.

'But how can we get in touch with them all?' asked Mr Bold, scratching his head. 'We don't have addresses for them, do we?'

'We don't,' said Mrs Bold. 'What a shame. I know where a couple of our dear friends live, like Sylvie and Bert, but not many of the others.'

'But you're the Bolds, remember?' pointed out Fergie. 'All animals know about you. I was told by an otter in Oz!'

'Hmmm,' said Mrs Bold, looking doubtful.

'We just need to alert all the animals, don't you see?' said Charlie.

'News of the party will spread like

wildfire,' said Annika. 'Animals can just pass on the message.'

'Brilliant idea!' said Mrs Bold.

'I love it!' said Mr Bold.

'Let's make the message this: It's Bobby and Betty's birthday. The Bolds are having a party in Bushy Park on 1st May – all friends welcome. Pass it on!' said Mrs Bold excitedly.

'I think it might just work. Thank you, Annika!' said Mr Bold.

News of the party was told to all and sundry in the animal world, wherever Mr and Mrs Bold and their friends encountered them. They began by telling the ducks at the pond, the deer in the park, and the cats, dogs and squirrels in Fairfield Road. Fergie flew on nightly expeditions and informed all the sheep, cows, horses and badgers in the countryside. Miranda the monkey swung up into the trees and told the birds, who then flew off all around spreading the word. And all the other animals in Fairfield Road told their friends, who told their friends, and so the news travelled far and wide. Similar to how things go 'viral' on the internet – but without the need for any computers. All the Bolds could do was hope that their old friends, wherever they might be living, heard about the party and were able to make it. But no one knew for sure.

As the day of the party approached, the excitement grew. And everyone had to be very careful not to let any word slip in front of the twins, of course.

Which reminds me of something I raised at the beginning of the story – the complex nature of the wrong thing versus the right thing. Is it wrong to keep secrets from your children and trick them, or is it right to give them the best surprise party ever? When I was a child I was asked what I'd like for my birthday. 'A bicycle,' I said. My mother shook her head sadly. 'I'm afraid we can't afford one. How about a yo-yo instead?' I said I didn't mind, although I really wanted a bike. Then, on the big day, my mother asked me to go and get a loaf of bread out of the freezer in the garage – and there it was! A bicycle! (Leaning against the freezer, not inside it, obvs.) So what are the rights and wrongs of all this? Should we let someone feel a bit sad for a while so that they can enjoy a great rush of happiness later on? I'll let you decide.

'I wonder if there will be enough cake to go round? Or too much?' pondered Mrs Bold, as she wrote 'HAPPY BIRTHDAY BETTY AND BOBBY!' in white icing on top of the cake the night before the big event.

'I do hope that is organic and the flour was from sustainable sources,' said Fifi primly.

'And gluten-free,' added Uncle Tony.

'Yes, of course!' Mrs Bold reassured her health-conscious friends.

Chapter

20

Finally the big day arrived. Sandwiches, crisps, samosas, fruit salad, dips, vegetable batons, peanuts, vegan sausage rolls, iced buns and a birthday cake were all placed carefully in a hamper, which was then balanced on top of the sturdy wheelbarrow that was already piled high with picnic rugs, cushions and folding chairs, all to be transported to Bushy Park.

'Seems like an awful lot of food,' said Mr Bold, licking his lips. 'How many people are we expecting, Amelia?'

'Who knows?' laughed Mrs Bold.

'The more the merrier!' said Uncle Tony, packing reusable cups into Miranda's pram.

It was important that everything was ready well before the twins arrived in the park, so Minnie waited for them at the park gate. Her job was to delay their arrival at the oak tree until a signal – a high-pitched cackle from Mr Bold – which would let her know the party was all set up and it was safe to bring the star guests there. When planning a surprise party, the 'surprise' bit is all-important.

'Hi, Betty, hi, Bobby!' said Minnie, when her friends arrived.

Minnie gave the twins a hug while making sure not to squash Walter, her little dog, who was asleep inside her cardigan.

'I made you "Happy Birthday" badges,' she added, pinning a big star on each of their chests.

'Thank you!' said Betty. 'At least someone's remembered.'

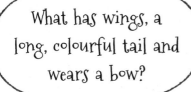

What has wings, a long, colourful tail and wears a bow?

A birthday pheasant!

'That's funny!' said Bobby, and he strode off in the direction of the oak tree.

Minnie jumped in front of him.

Er, what did the
hermit crab do on
his birthday?

He shellebrated!

Betty chuckled,
but walked around
Minnie.

'No, wait!' said Minnie,
playing for time.

What kind of party
game do rabbits
like most?

'Musical hares, I expect,' said Bobby, now slightly cross. 'Let's get going. We don't want to miss the opening ceremony of the den, do we?'

'There's plenty of time,' said Minnie.

Knock, knock!

Betty rolled her eyes, reluctant to join in. 'Look,' she said. 'We don't want to hear any more jokes right now. OK? We're not in the mood. Everyone except you has forgotten our birthday and—' But just then Mr Bold's high-pitched cackle was heard.

'Is that Dad?' asked Bobby.

'Yes,' said Betty. 'Let's just get to the oak tree.'

'Yes,' agreed Minnie, relieved. 'Let's.'

At the oak tree everything was ready. All the guests had been instructed to lie low in the long grass and ferns and hide, making no noise whatsoever. Just Mr and Mrs Bold were standing by the entrance to the den, looking as casual as possible, when the twins and Minnie arrived. Uncle Tony was pretending to snooze in a deckchair with Miranda asleep on his shoulder and Mr McNumpty appeared to be occupied with tying a bit of ribbon across the den entrance and didn't look up.

'Hi, Minnie dear,' said Mrs Bold cheerily. 'How are you today?'

'I'm fine,' said Minnie, as casually as she could.

'That's good,' replied Mrs Bold, giving the little girl a pat on the shoulder. 'Nice sunny day, isn't it? Oh, what lovely badges, Betty and Bobby. What do they say?' She leaned forward to read. Then said calmly: 'Oh, of course. Silly me. I almost forgot . . . is it YOUR BIRTHDAY TODAY?'

No sooner were the words spoken than suddenly animals of every shape and size rose up out of the ferns, some holding bunting and balloons, some pulling party poppers and all wearing party hats and holding presents.

'SURPRISE!' they boomed together. 'HAPPY BIRTHDAY, BOBBY AND BETTY!'

And it *was* a surprise! Betty almost jumped out of her skin. Bobby hooted with delight.

'Oh, wow! I don't believe this!' he cried. 'We thought you'd forgotten.'

'Never!' said his dad.

'This is just amazing!' said Betty. 'Look – just look who's here!'

HAPPY BIRTHDAY
BOBBY AND BETTY!

Apart from Annika, Charlie, Fergie, Fifi and Samir with their pups, there were lots of familiar faces who crowded around to offer birthday wishes. Some climbed the branches of the oak to see better and call out their greetings, and those with wings flew up in the sky.

The air was full of cries of 'Happy birthday, Betty and Bobby!'

'Remember us?' said Minty Boy and Gangster's Moll, the two racehorses whom the Bolds had rescued and helped a while back.

'Congratulations!' said Sylvie and Bert, the two loved-up foxes.

'Couldn't miss your special day!' said Roger the sheep.

'Yoo-hoo!' said Craig the wild boar, another old guest.

'Snappy birthday!' snapped Snappy the goose.

'Blessings on you, my children!' prayed Sister Paulina the otter.

'H-h-happy birth-d-day!' puffed Pam the puffing puffin, who'd flown all the way from Cornwall.

'Have a grrrreat day!' purred Bertha the cougar.

'Wishing you joy, dear Betty and Bobby!' called Hector the cuckoo from his perch above.

'Have a woofy birthday!' barked Taxi the Jack Russell, before running off to chase Charlie in circles around the park.

There were cards and messages too, from those who *couldn't* make it to Bushy Park: Grandma Imamu, Sheila the crocodile, Galileo the dolphin, and Jeffrey the ape man.

As the twins greeted all the guests one by one, Mr McNumpty put some pop music on the ghetto blaster and Mr and Mrs Bold opened the hamper and began to pass round the delicious, wholesome food and glasses of home-made lemonade.

And so the BIG surprise party took off and then went on. And on and on.

There was a pause when the twins, as guests of honour, were asked to cut the ceremonial ribbon and declare the new, ultra-green den open.

'We hope Annika, Charlie and Fergie will be happy in their lovely new home,' said Betty.

'As happy as *we* are today,' added Bobby.

'We now declare this den open for residence!'

Everyone cheered and took it in turns to enter the burrow and admire all the smart, eco-friendly features and fittings. Particularly appreciated was the Home sweet home! sign that Mr Bold had made from an old piece of wood, the letters carved with his own teeth.

Later, just as things were peaking, Mrs Bold presented the twins with their special chocolate birthday cake. There were lots of stars and spangles on the top and, of course, ten candles.

'Make a wish!' Minnie instructed her friends. Betty and Bobby closed their eyes, took a deep breath and blew out all the candles on the first attempt. You must never tell anyone your birthday wish, but I know that the twins wished for everyone's birthday to be as happy as theirs – and for the earth to heal and be well again. (I, for one, am very hopeful that their wish will come true.)

'Hurrah!' everyone cheered.

'*Et maintenant*,' said Fifi, 'I wish for everyone to join me in singing "Bon Anniversaire"! In B-flat, please!'

Everyone of every species (and, despite instructions, in a variety of keys) sang:

'HAPPY BIRTHDAY TO YOU,
HAPPY BIRTHDAY TO YOU,
HAPPY BIRTHDAY
DEAR BETTY AND BOBBY . . .
HAPPY BIRTHDAY TO YOU!'

After that cacophony there was fun, laughter, games, singing, dancing, chatter and even a few tears of happiness from Mrs Bold. As the party began to wind down and the spring sun started to set in the sky, Bobby, Betty and Minnie went around collecting and sorting all the rubbish into big, biodegradable sacks, and thanking all their guests for coming and making their tenth birthday so special.

'The best party ever!' said Fifi, as she and Samir gently groomed their contented pups. 'And a wonderful end to my visit home.'

'You're not leaving, are you?' asked Betty.

'Soon, *mon petit*,' said Fifi. 'We 'ave been discussing our future.' She looked affectionately at Samir. 'We are to return to Egypt. Samir will stay at home with our babies and I will resume my singing career. The public demand to hear me sing

and I cannot deny them this pleasure!'

'But you will come back again one day?' asked Bobby.

'*Mais oui!*' declared the French poodle passionately. 'Wherever life might take me, my heart belongs with the Bolds. Always and for ever!'

And that, dear readers, goes for me as well.

THE END

MR BOLD'S JOKES

Why did the jellybean go to school?
To become a Smartie!

'I used to work in a recycling centre, crushing cans.'
'Did you really?'
'Yes. But I had to give it up. It was soda pressing.'

How does a penguin build its house?
Igloos it together!

What kind of flowers grow on your face?
Tu-lips!

Why did the ant smell?
Because he didn't wear deodorANT!

What do you call an ant who skips school?
A truANT!

Where do ants go on holiday?
FrANTS!

What do you call the tallest ant in the world?
A giANT!

How did Noah see in the dark?
He used floodlights!

Why were the Middle Ages called the Dark Ages?
Because there were too many knights!

How do bees get to school?
On the school buzz!

Why is a school like an old bus?
Because it's full of nuts and has a crank up front!

What did the French skeleton call his friend?
Bone ami!

What do baby footballers do in their sleep?
Dribble!

What do you call a cow on a trampoline?
A milkshake!

Why didn't the nose want to go to school?
Because he was tired of being picked on!

How do you make an octopus laugh?
With ten tickles!

What do you call a dog detective?
Sherlock Bones!

How many skunks does it take to make a big stink?
Quite a PHEW!

What do you call a flying skunk?
A smell-icopter!

What did the watch say to the clock?
"Hour you doing!"

Have you heard the joke about the skunk and the camping trip?
Never mind, it really stinks!

What did the beaver say to the tree?
Been nice gnawing you!

What do you get when you cross a phone with a dog?
A golden receiver!

What do puppies eat for breakfast?
Pooched eggs!

Why did the hyena get heartburn after eating birthday cake?
He forgot to take off the candles!

Why did the rubber chicken cross the road?
To stretch his legs!

Why does Santa always go down the chimney?
Because it soots him!

Knock, knock!
Who's there?
Gus.
Gus who?
Gus whose birthday it is today!

What has wings, a long, colourful tail and wears a bow?
A birthday pheasant!

What did the hermit crab do on his birthday?
He shellebrated!

What kind of birthday party game do rabbits like most?
Musical hares

Knock, knock,
Who's there?
Dishes.
Dishes who?
Dishes a nice place you've got here!

What did the big tree say to the little tree?
Leaf me alone!

What does a cloud wear under his raincoat?
Thunderwear!

Where does a caterpillar buy his clothes?
A cater-logue!

What's a caterpillar's favourite weapon?
A cater-pult

What is the definition of a caterpillar?
A worm in a fur coat!

What do you get if you cross a clock with a chicken?
A cluck!

What did the robber say to the clock?
Hands up!

Why can't dogs drive?
Because they can't find a
barking space!

Why did the belt go
to jail?
Because he held up a
pair of trousers!

What kind of shoes do
frogs wear?
Open toad!

Why did Grandma put
wheels on her rocking
chair?
Because she wanted
to rock and roll.

Knock, knock!
Who's there?
Tyrone.
Tyrone who?
Tyrone shoelaces!

Knock, knock!
Who's there?
Olive.
Olive who?
Olive next door.

Knock, knock!
Who's there?
Nana.
Nana who?
Nana your business!

What animal do you
look like when you
get in the bath?
A little bear!

How do you know there's a monster in your bath?
You can't get the shower curtain closed!

What kind of table can you eat?
A vege-table!

Which birds steal soap from the bath?
Robber ducks

What did the pencil sharpener say to the pencil?
Stop going round in circles and get to the point!

What vegetables do librarians like?
Quiet peas!

What do elves learn in school?
The elf-abet!

What's red and flies and wobbles at the same time?
A jelly-copter!

How do you make a milkshake?
Give it a good scare!

How do chimps make toast?
Under the gorilla!

What do you get when dinosaurs crash their cars?
Tyrannosaurus wrecks!

Why was the broom late?
He overswept!

Where do chimps get their gossip from?
The ape vine!

What do you call a baby monkey?
A chimp off the old block!

What do you call an exploding monkey?
A bab-boom!

What's the best time to see gorillas in the wild?
Ape-ril!

What type of tree fits in your hand?
A palm tree!

What's the difference between a schoolteacher and a train?
A teacher says, "Spit out your gum", and the train says, "Chew, chew, chew!"

How do you know when a yacht is happy?
When it hugs the shore!

What has four wheels and flies?
A rubbish truck!

When Julian Clary isn't having a silly time dressing up and telling jokes on stage, he loves to be at home with his pets. He has lots of them: dogs, cats, ducks and chickens. His life-long love of animals inspired him to tell a story about what would happen if they pretended to be like us. Julian loves going on tour reading his books aloud to children and animals around the country.

David Roberts always loved to draw and paint as a child, and when he grew up his talents took him all the way to Hong Kong where he got a job making beautiful hats. But he always wanted to illustrate children's books, and so he came back to England to work with the finest authors in the land. David loves drawing animals and clothes and hats, so what could be better than a book about animals *in* clothes and hats?

Have you read them all?

Join the Bolds on lots more
'howling' adventures!

  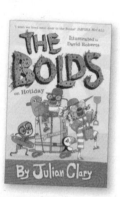